VALMOUTH

VALMOUTH

RONALD FIRBANK

DUCKWORTH

This impression 1977

First published in England 1919

Gerald Duckworth & Co. Ltd.
The Old Piano Factory
43 Gloucester Crescent, London NW1

ISBN 0 7156 1093 7 (cased)
ISBN 0 7156 1097 X (paper)

Printed in Great Britain
by Unwin Brothers Limited,
The Gresham Press, Old Woking, Surrey

I

DAY was drooping on a fine evening in March as a brown barouche passed through the wrought-iron gates of Hare-Hatch House on to the open highway.

Beneath the crepuscular, tinted sky the country-side stretched away, interspersed with hamlets, meads and woods, towards low, loosely engirdling hills, that rose up against the far horizon with a fine monastic roll.

Although it was but the third month of the year, yet, from a singular softness of the air, already the trees were in full, fresh leaf. Along the hedgerows hawthorns were in bloom, while the many wild flowers by the roadside scented in fitful whiffs an invigorating, caressing breeze.

Seated immediately behind the coachman in the shell-like carriage was a lady no longer young. Her fragile features, long and pointed, were swathed, quasi-biblically, in a striped Damascus shawl that looked Byzantine, at either side of which escaped a wisp of red, crimped hair. Her big, wide eyes, full of innocent, child-like wonder, were set off by arched auburn brows that in the twilight seemed almost to be phosphorescent.

By her side reclined a plump, placidish person, whose face was half concealed beneath a white-lace coalscuttle hat.

" Some *suppose* . . . while *others*——; again, I'm told . . . And in *any case*, my dear! " The voice came droning in a monotonous, sing-song way.

Facing the ladies a biretta'd priest appeared to be perusing a little, fat, black, greasy book of prayers

7

which he held aslant so as to catch the light. Every now and then he would raise a cold, hypnotic eye above the margin of his page towards the ladies *vis-à-vis*.

" Of whom are you so unkindly speaking, Mrs. Thoroughfare? " he inquired at length.

The head beneath the coalscuttle-shaped hat drooped confused.

" I? Oh, my dear Father——! "

" Yes? my dear child? . . ."

" I was only telling Mrs. Hurstpierpoint how——"

Mrs. Hurstpierpoint—the dowager of the gleaming brows—leaned forward all at once in the carriage and pulled the checkstring attached to her footman's arm.

" Benighted idiot! " she exclaimed.

The fellow turned towards his mistress a melancholy, dreamy face that had something of a *quia multum amavit* expression in its wizen whiteness, and raised stiffly to a frayed silk cockade a long, bare hand.

" Didn't I say, blunt-headed booby, to Valmouth? "

" To Valmouth? "

" By way of Fleet. *Pardon*, Thoroughfare," the dowager murmured, " you were saying——"

" Evil, evil, evil," her companion returned. " Nothing but slander, wickedness and lies. *N'est-ce pas*, Father Colley? "

" What is your book, Father Colley-Mahoney? " Mrs. Hurstpierpoint asked.

" St. Stanislaus-Kostka, my child."

" Kostka——! It sounds like one of those islands, those savage islands, where my big, handsome, strong —*and* delicate!—darling Dick stopped at once, just to write to his old mother," Mrs. Thoroughfare declared.

" Where is he now, Eliza? "

" Off the coast of Jamaica. His *ship*——" she broke

8

off as a voice full and flexible rose suddenly from behind a burgeoning quincunx of thorns:

" I heard the voice of Jesus say-y-y! Yahoo, to
heel. Bad dog."

" It's that crazy Corydon," Mrs. Thoroughfare
blinked.

" Which, dear, crazy? "

" David Tooke—the brother, you know, of that
extraordinarily extraordinary girl."

" Thoroughfare."

" Father? "

" That tongue."

" The last time Dick was at Hare, I thought——"

" *Meet me in glow-ry by the gate o' pearl*. Hi, Douce! "
the voice irrelevantly veered, as, over a near meadow,
barking lustily, sprang a shaggy sheep-dog. " Hi,
Douce boy! . . . Doucey! Douce! "

The Priest pulled the light merino carriage rug
higher about his knees.

" How," he addressed Mrs. Hurstpierpoint, whose
chevelure in the diminishing daylight was taking on
almost the appearance of an aureole, " how if the
glorious Virgin required you to take this young fellow
under your wing? "

Mrs. Hurstpierpoint bent thoughtfully her eyes to
the somewhat " phallic " passementerie upon her
shawl.

" For the sake, I presume," she queried, " of his
soul? "

" Precisely."

" But is he ripe? " Mrs. Thoroughfare wondered.

" Ripe? "

" I *mean*——"

There was a busy silence.

Descending a narrow tree-lined lane the carriage
passed into a leisurely winding road, bounded by
market-gardens and the River Val. Through a belt

9

of osier and alder Valmouth, with its ancient bridge and great stone church, that from the open country had the scheming look of an ex-cathedral, showed a few lit lamps.

Mrs. Thoroughfare twittered.

" I did require a ribbon, a roughish ribbon," she announced, " and to call as well at the music-shop for those Chopin sonatas."

" A 'roughish' ribbon? " Father Colley-Mahoney echoed in searching tones. " And pray, might I ask, what is that? "

" It's—— Oh, Father."

" Is it silk? Or satin? Or is it velvet? Is it," he conscientiously pressed, " something rose-leafy? Something lilac? . . . Eh? Or sky-blue, perhaps? . . . Insidious child! "

" Insidious, Father? "

" Prevaricating."

" Pax, Father," Mrs. Thoroughfare beseeched.

Father Colley-Mahoney gazed moodily above the floppy fabric of her hat at an electric two-seater that was endeavouring to forge by the barouche from behind.

As it came abreast of it the occupants, a spruce, middle-aged man, and a twinkling negress, who clasped in her arms a something that looked to be an india-rubber coil, respectfully bowed.

" Dr. Dee, and la Yajñavalkya! "

" Those appliances of hers——; that she flaunts! "

" In massaging her ' cases,' " Mrs. Thoroughfare *sotto-voce* said, " I'm told she has a trick of—um."

" Oh? "

" And of—um! "

" Indeed? "

" So poor Marie Wilks' nurse told my maid . . ."

" When," Father Colley-Mahoney murmured, *"was* Miss Wilks a hundred? "

"Only last week."

"Nowadays," Mrs. Hurstpierpoint commented, "around Valmouth centenarians will be soon as common as peas!"

"The air," Mrs. Thoroughfare sniffed, "there's no air to compare to it."

"For the sake of veracity, I should be tempted to qualify that."

"I fancy I'm not the only one, Father, to swear by Valmouth air!"

"Valmouth air, Valmouth air."

"At the Strangers' Hotel," Mrs. Thoroughfare giddily went on, "it seems there's not a single vacant bed. No; nor settle either. . . . Victor Vatt, the delicate *paysagiste*—the English Corot—came yester-day, and Lady Parvula de Panzoust was to arrive to-day."

"I was her bridesmaid some sixty years ago—and she was no girl then," Mrs. Hurstpierpoint smiled.

"She stands, I fear, poor thing, now, for something younger than she looks."

"Fie, Thoroughfare!"

"Fie, Father?"

"*La jeunesse—hélas,*" Mrs. Hurstpierpoint softly said, "*n'a qu'un temps.*"

Father Colley-Mahoney looked absently away towards the distant hills whose outlines gleamed elusively beneath the rising moon.

Here and there, an orchard, in silhouette, showed all in black blossom against an extravagant sky.

II

TROTTING before his master, the fire-flies singing his tale, ran the watch-dog Douce. From the humid earth beneath his firm white paws the insects clamoured zing-zing-zing. Nuzzling intently the ground, sampling the pliant grasses, he would return from time to time to menace some lawless calf or cow.

Following a broken trackway through the deserted corn-land, the herd filed lazily towards the town in a long, close queue. Tookes Farm, or Abbots Farm, as it indifferently was called, whither they now were bent, lay beneath the decayed walls of St. Veronica, the oldest church in the town. Prior to the Reformation the farm buildings (since rebuilt and considerably dwindled) had appertained, like much of the glebe-land around Valmouth, to the Abbots of St. Veronica, when at the confiscation of the monasteries by the Crown one Thierry Monfaulcon Tooke, tennis-master to the Court of King Henry VIII, feinting to injure himself one day while playing with the royal princesses, had been offered by Henry, through their touching entreaties " in consideration of his mishap," the Abbey Farm of St. Veronica's, then recently vacated by the monks; from which same Thierry (in the space of only six generations) the estate had passed to his descendants of the present time. Now in the bluey twilight as seen from the fields the barns and outhouses appeared really to be more capacious than the farm itself. With its whitewashed walls and small-paned latticed windows it showed poorly enough between the two sumptuous wheat-ricks that stood reared on either side. Making their way across the long cobble bridge that spanned the Val, the cattle turned into an elm-lined lane that conducted to the farmyard gates, where, pottering expectantly, was a tiny boy.

At a bark from Douce he swung wide a creaking cross-barred gate overspread by a thorn-tree all in flower.

With lethargic feet the animals stumbled through, proceeding in an automatic way to a strip of water at the far end of the yard into which they turned. By the side of it ran an open hangar upheld by a score of rough tarred posts. Against these precocious calves were wont as a rule to rub their crescent horns. Within showed a wagon or two, and a number of roosting doves.

Depositing his scrip in the outhouse the cowherd glanced around.

" Where's Thetis got? " he asked, addressing the small boy, who, brandishing a broken rhubarb-leaf, was flitting functionarily about.

" Thetis? . . . She's," he hopped, " standing in the river."

" What's she standing there for? "

" Nothing."

" . . . Must I thrash you, Bobby Jolly? "

" Oh, don't, David."

" Then answer me quick."

" When the tide flows up from Spadder Bay she pretends it binds her to the sea. Where her sweetheart is. Her b-betrothed. . . . Away in the glorious tropics."

" 'Od! You're a simple one; you are! "

" Me? "

" Aye, you."

" Don't be horrid, David, to me. . . . You mustn't be. It's bad enough quite without."

" 'Od."

" What with granny——"

" She'll not be here for long."

" I don't think she'll die just yet."

" It's a cruel climate," the young man ruefully said, looking impatiently up through his eyelashes towards the stars.

It was one of the finest nights imaginable. The moon reigned full in the midst of a cloudless sky. From the thorn-tree by the gate the sound of a bird singing floated down exuberantly through the leaves.

" Aye, cruel," he muttered, shouldering a pitch-fork and going out into the yard. As he did so the church clock rang out loudly in the air above.

" Shall I find 'ee, Thetis? "

" Nay. Maybe I'll go myself."

Beyond the low yard wall gleamed the river, divided from the farm by a narrow garden parcelled out in vegetables and flowers.

A cindered pathway sloping between spring-lettuces and rows of early tulips whose swollen calyxes, milk-white, purple and red, probed superbly the moon-mist, led to the water's edge where, clinging to the branches of a pollard-willow, a girl was gently swaying with the tide. On her head, slightly thrown back, and slashed all over with the shadow of the willow leaves, was perched a small sailor's toque adorned with a spread gannet's wing that rose up venturesomely from the ribboned cord. Her light print frock, care-lessly caught about her, revealed her bare legs below the knees.

The cowherd paused hesitant.

" Thetis—! " he called.

Self-absorbed, wrapped in enchanting fancies, she turned: " H'lo? "

" Come in now."

" I shan't."

" Come in, Thetis."

" I won't. I will not."

" You'll catch your death! "

" What of it? "

14

" The-tis. . . ."

With a laugh, she whisked further out into the stream.

Through her parted fingers, in microscopic wavelets, it swept, all moon-plashed from the sea.

Laughing, she bent her lips to the briny water.

III

In a little back sitting-room overlooking the church-yard Granny Tooke, in a high rush-chair, was sharing a basin of milk with the cat.

It was her " Vibro day," a day when a sound like wild-bees swarming made ghostly music through the long-familiar room. Above the good green trees the venerable wood dial of St. Veronica's great clock informed her that, in the normal course of things, Madam Yajñavalkya and her instruments should already be on their way.

" Was there ever a cat like ye for milk, Tom? " the old lady wondered, setting down the half-emptied bowl on the whatnot beside her, and following with a poulterer's discerning eye the careless movements of the farm pigeons as they preened themselves on the long gross gargoyles of the church.

Once, long ago, in that same building she had stood a round-cheeked bride. Alas for life's little scars! . . . Now, all wrapped up like a moulting canary, her dun, lean face was fuller of wrinkles than a withered russet. Nevertheless, it was good still to be alive! Old Mrs. Tooke sighed with self-complacence as her glance took in the grave-ground, in whose dark, doughy soil so many former cronies lay asleep. It was a rare treat for her to be able, without any effort, to witness from time to time a neighbour's last impressive pomps; to watch " the gentlemen " in their tall town tiles " bearing up poor fellows"; to join (unseen in her high rush-chair, herself in carpet-slippers) in the long, lugubrious hymn; to respire through the window chinks of her room the faint exotic perfume of aromatic flowers from a ground all white with wreaths.

16

But, to-day, there were no obsequies to observe at all.

Through the window glass she could see Maudie and Maidie Comedy, daughters of Q. Comedy, Esq., the local estate agent and auctioneer, amusing themselves by making daisy ᵔhains by the mortuary door, while within the church some one—evidently not the vicar's sister—was casting the stale contents of an altar-vase through a clerestory-window (sere sweet by sweet), quite callous of passers-by.

Mrs. Tooke blew pensively the filmy skin forming upon her milk. A long sunbeam lighting up the what-not caused the great copper clasp of her Bible to emit a thousand playful sparks, bringing to her notice somewhat glaringly a work of fiction that assuredly asn't hers. . . . Extending a horny hand towards it, she had hardly made out a line when her grand-daughter looked languorously in.

" Your towels are nicely steaming," she said, resting her prepossessing, well-formed face against the polished woodwork of the door.

Mrs. Tooke coughed drily.

" So far," she murmured, " Mrs. Yaj ha'n't come."

" It's such a splendid morning."

" Where's David? "

" He went out early with the barley-mow."

" Any orders? "

" The hotel only—extra butter."

" Be sure to say it's risen. Butter and eggs," Mrs. Tooke dramatically declared, " have gone up. And while you're at the Strangers' you might propose a pair of pigeons, or two, to the cook."

Miss Tooke turned yearningly her head.

" You'd think," she faltered, " they were seagulls, poor darlings, up there so white."

" If only I could get about the place." Mrs. Tooke restively pursued, " as once I did."

"Maybe with warmer weather here you will. This very night the old sweetbrier tree came out. The old sweetbrier! And none of us thought it could."

"In heaven's name," her grandmother peevishly snapped, "don't let me hear you talk of thinking. A more feather-brained girl there never lived."

"I often think, at any rate," Miss Tooke replied, "I was born for something *more brilliant* than waiting on you."

"Impudent baggage! Here, take it—before I tear it."

"My library book?"

"Pah to the library. I wish there was none."

Miss Tooke shrugged slightly her shoulders.

"There's Douce barking," she said, "I expect it's Mrs. Yaj."

And in effect a crisp rat-a-tat on the yard-door gate was followed by a majestical footfall on the stair.

"Devil dog, pariah! Let go of me," a voice came loudly drifting from below ; a voice, large, deep, buoyant, of a sonorous persuasiveness, issuing straight from the entrails of the owner.

Mrs. Tooke had a passing palpitation.

"Put the chain on Douce, and make ready the thingamies!" she commanded, as Mrs. Yajñavalkya, wreathed in smiles, sailed briskly into the room.

She had a sheeny handkerchief rolled round and round her head, a loud-dyed petticoat and a tartan shawl.

"Forgive me I dat late," she began. "But I just dropped off to sleep again—like a little chile—after de collation."

"Howsomever!" Mrs. Tooke exclaimed.

"Ah! de clients, Mrs. Tooke!" The negress beamed. "Will you believe it now, but I was on my legs this morning before four! . . . Hardly was there a light in the sky when an old gentleman he send for me to de Strangers' Hotel."

18

Mrs. Tooke professed astonishment.

"I understood you never 'took' a gentleman," she said.

"No more do I, Mrs. Tooke. Only," Mrs. Yajñavalkya comfortably sighed. "I like to relieve my own sex."

"Up at four!" Mrs. Tooke archly quavered.

"And how do you find yourself to-day, Mrs. Tooke? How is dat sciatica ob yours?"

"To be open with you, Mrs. Yaj, I feel to-day as if all my joints want oiling!"

"What you complain ob, Mrs. Tooke, is nothing but stiffness—due very largely from want ob par. Or (as we Eastern women sometimes say) from want ob vim. Often de libber you know it get sluggish. But it will pass. . . . I shall not let—you hear me?—I shall not let you slip through my fingers: oh no: your life wif me is so precious."

"I can't hope to last very much longer, Mrs. Yaj, anyway, I suppose."

"That is for me to say, Mrs. Tooke," the imperious woman murmured, beginning to remove, by way of preliminary, the numerous glittering rings with which her hands were laden.

"Heysey-ho!" the old lady self-solicitously sighed, "she's getting on."

"And so's de time, Mrs. Tooke! But have no fear. Waited for as I am by a peeress ob distinction, I would never rush my art, especially wif you. No; oh no. You, my dear, are my most beautiful triumph! Have I not seen your precious life fluttering away, spent? Den at a call . . . I . . . wif my science—wif dese two hand have I not restored you to all de world's delights?"

"Delights," Mrs. Tooke murmured, going off into a mournful key. "Since the day my daughter-in-law —Charlotte Carpster that was—died in child-bed, and my great, bonny wild-oat of a son destroyed himself in a fit of remorse, there's been nothing but trouble for me."

"And how is your young grandchild's erot-o-maniah, Mrs. Tooke? Does it increase?"

"God knows, Mrs. Yaj, what it does."

"We Eastern women," Mrs. Yajñavalkya declared, drawing off what perhaps was once her union-ring, "never take lub serious. And w'y is dis, Mrs. Tooke? —Because it is so serious!"

"Love in the East Mrs. Yaj, I presume, is *only* feasible indoors?"

"Nobody bothers, Mrs. Tooke. Common couples wif no place else often go into de jungle."

"Those cutting winds of yours must be a bar to courting."

"Our cutting winds! It is you who have de cutting winds. . . . It is not us. . . . No; oh no. In de East it is joy, heat!"

"Then where do those wicked blasts come from?"

"Never you mind now, Mrs. Tooke, but just cross dose two dear knees ob yours, and do wot I bid you. . . . Dis incipient pass," the beneficent woman explained, seating herself in the window-bench facing Mrs. Tooke's arm-chair, "is a daisy. And dat is sure, O Allah la Ilaha," she gurgled, "but I shall have you soon out in de open air again, I hope, and den you shall visit *me*. . . . De white acacia-tree in my back garden is something so beautiful dis year; at dis season it even eclipse my holly. . . . Ah, Mrs. Tooke! Whenebber I look at a holly it put me in mind ob my poor Mustapha again. It has just de same playful prickle as a mastodon's moustache. Husband and wife ought to cling together, Mrs. Tooke; if only for de sake ob de maintenance; it's hard often, my dear, for one in de professional-way to make both ends meet; clients don't always pay; you may rub your arms off

20

for some folk (and include all de best specifics), but never a dollar will you see! "

" Howsomever," Mrs. Tooke exclaimed, eyeing mistrustfully her granddaughter, who had re-entered the room unobtrusively with the towels.

She had a sun-hat on, equipped to go out.

" Where are you off, so consequential? " the old lady interrogatively said.

" Nowhere in particular."

" In that big picture-hat—? Don't tell me! "

" I shall be back again, I dare say, before you're ready," Miss Tooke replied, withdrawing on tiptoe from the room.

" Dat enlarged heart should be seen to, Mrs. Tooke. Do persuade her now to try my sitz-baths. I sell ze twelve tickets ver cheap—von dozen for only five shillings," the young girl could hear the mulattress murmur as she closed the door.

Taking advantage of her grandame's hour of treatment, it was her habit, whenever this should occur, to sally forth for a stroll. Often she would slip off to Spadder Bay and lie upon the beach there, her pale cheek pressed to the wet sea-shingle; oftener perhaps she would wander towards Hare-Hatch House in the hope of a miraculous return.

This morning her feet were attracted irresistibly towards Hare.

Crossing the churchyard into the Market Square, where, above booths and shops and the flowered façade of the Strangers' Hotel, towered the statue of John Baptist Daleman, b. 1698, ob. 1803, Valmouth's illustrious son, Miss Tooke sauntered slowly across the old brick bridge that spanned the Val. Here, beneath a cream canvas sunshade traced at the borders with narrow lines of blue, sat Victor Vatt, the landscape artist, a colour-box upon his knee. At either side of him crouched a pupil—young men who, as they watched the veteran painter's hand, grew quite hot and red and religious-looking.

Bearing on, Miss Tooke branched off into an unfrequented path that led along the river-reach, between briers and little old stunted pollard-willows, towards Hare. Kingfishers emeralder than the grass passed like dream-birds along the bank. Wrapped in fancy, walking in no great hurry, she would pause, from time to time, to stand and droop, and dream and die. Between the sodden, creaking bark of pollard-willows, weeping for sins not theirs, the sea, far off, showed pulsating in the sun.

> " I loved a man
> And he sailed away,
> Ah hé, ah hé,"

she sang.

From Valmouth to Hare-Hatch House was reckoned a longish mile. Half buried in cedar woods, it stood on high ground above the valley of the Val, backed by the bluish hills of Spadder Tor. Ascending a zigzag track she entered a small fir plantation that was known by most people thereabouts as Jackdaw Wood; but, more momentously, for her it was " *the* " wood. How sweetly he had kissed her in its kindly gloom. . . . On those dead fir-needles hand in hand, his bright eyes bent to hers (those dear entrancing eyes that held the glamour of foreign seaports in them), he had told her of her goddess namesake of Greece, of the nereid Thetis, the sister of Calypso, and the mother of Achilles, the most paradoxical of all the Greeks. On these dead fir-needles he had told her of his ship—the *Sesostris*—and of his middy-chum, Jack Whorwood, who was not much over fifteen, and the youngest hand on board. " That little lad," he had said, with a peculiar smile that revealed his regular pointed teeth, " that little lad, upon a cruise, is, to me, what Patroclus was to Achilles, and even more."

Ruminating, she roamed along, brushing the rose-spiked self-heal and the red-thimbled fox-gloves with her dress. Upon a fitful breeze a wailing repeated cry of a peacock smote like music on her ear and drew her on. Striking the highway beyond the little copse she skirted the dark iron palings enclosing Hare. Through the armorial great gates—open as if expectant—the house lay before her across a stretch of drive.

Halting she stood, lost in amorous conjectures, surveying with hungry eyes the sun-bleached, mute façade.

Oh, which amongst those tiers of empty windows lit his room?

Above each tall window was a carved stone mask. Strange chiselled faces, singularly saturnine . . . that laughed and leered and frowned. His room perhaps faced the other way? Her eyes swept the long pseudo-classic pile. Above the gaunt grey slates showed the tops of the giant cryptomerias upon the lawn.

She had never penetrated there.

To one side of it on a wooded hillock rose a garden temple open to the winds, its four white columns uplifting each a bust.

Beneath the aerial cupola three people at present were seated, engaged in tranquil chat.

Transfixed, Miss Tooke considered them. She was there, in spirit, too, " holding her own," as her grand-mother would have said, with those two patrician women and the priest.

IV

THEY were ringing the angelus. Across the darkling meadows, from the heights of Hare, the tintinnabulation sounded mournfully, penetrating the curl-wreathed tympanums of Lady Parvula de Panzoust.

"There's the dinner-bell, coachman!" her ladyship impatiently exclaimed, speaking through the ventilator of her cab. "Please to get on."

Whipping up his horse with an inventive expletive, the driver started forward at a trot.

Lady Parvula relaxed.

The invitation to dinner at Hare-Hatch House had included her daughter, the Hon. Gilda Vintage, as well; a fair girl whose vast fortune as sole heiress of the late Lord de Panzoust caused her to be considered one of the most tempting present *partis* in the land. Bring Gilda, Mrs. Hurstpierpoint had written to Lady Parvula, "so that, not unlikely," her ladyship blissfully mused, "Captain Thoroughfare will be there!"

Captain Thoroughfare.

There were rumours, to be sure, he was above Love.

Lady Parvula studied dreamily her hands. (She had long, psychic, pallid, amorous fingers, much puffed at the tips and wrinkled.)

"Oh, how I wish *I* were!" she reflected. "But that is something I never was. . . . Who was that I saw by the ditch just now? *Quel joli garçon!* Quite—as Byron said of D'Orsay—a '*cupidon déchaîné.*' . . . Such a build. And such a voice! Especially, when he called his horrid dog to heel. *I heard the voice of Jesus say, yahoo—yahoo, bad dog!*"

24

Lady Parvula threw a little palpitating smile towards the evening star.

"He must be mine," she murmured, "in my manner . . . in my way . . . I always told my dear late Lord I could love a shepherd—peace be to his soul!"

A grey-haired manservant, and a couple of under-footmen wearing the violet vestments of the House-basilica (and which for moral reasons they were requested of an evening to retain), were meanwhile awaiting the arrival of the Valmouth cab, while conversing in undertones among themselves as servants sometimes do.

"Dash their wigs!" the elderly man exclaimed.

"What's the thorn, Mr. ffines?" his colleague, a lad with a face gemmed lightly over with spots, pertly queried.

"The thorn, George?"

"Tell us."

"I'd sooner go round my beads."

"Mrs. Hurst cut compline, for a change, to-night."

". . . She's making a studied toilet, so I hear."

"Gloria! Gloria! Gloria!"

"Dissenter."

"What's wrong with Nit?"

The younger footman flushed.

"Father Mahoney sent for me to his room again," he answered.

"What, *again?*"

"Catch me twice——"

"*Veni cum me in terra coelabus!*"

"S-s-s-s-s-s-sh."

"*Et lingua . . . semper.*"

"On the whole," the butler said, "I preferred Père Ernest."

"And so did half the maids."

"Although his brilliance here was as you may say wasted."

25

" 'Pon my word! It's a deadly awful place."

" With the heir-presumptive so much away it's bound to be slow and quiet."

" Why," George gurgled, " the Captain should be heir of Hare I never could make out! "

" Mr. Dick's dead father," Mr. ffines replied, " was a close relative of Mrs. Hurst."

" The Admiral? "

" And it was as good as a combination . . ." he further explained, " only he was too poor. And things fell out otherwise."

" There'd be a different heir, I s'pose, if missis married ag'in? "

" 'Tisn't likely. Why she'll soon be a centenarian herself."

" You've only to change her plate," Nit, with acumen, said, " to feel she's there."

" So I should hope! "

" And as to Father Colley. My! How he do press! "

The servitors waxed silent, each lost in introspection, until the rattle of the Valmouth cab announced the expected guest.

Alighting like some graceful exotic bird from the captivity of a dingy cage, Lady Parvula de Panzoust hovered a moment before the portal as much to manipulate her draperies, it seemed, as to imbreathe the soft sweet air.

The sky was abloom with stars. . . .

In the faint elusive light flitter-mice were whirling about the mask-capped windows, hurtling the wind-sown wallflowers embedded in the fissure of each saturnine-hewn face.

" Come back for me again by ten o'clock, remember," her ladyship commanded her coachman, prior to following the amaranthine skirts of the two footmen into the house.

Passing through the bleak penumbra of the hall and

26

along a corridor bristling with horns of every description, she was shown into a deep, T-shaped, panelled room profusely hung with pictures.

There seemed at present to be no one in it.

" The mistress, I presume, is with the scourge," the butler announced, peering impassably around.

Lady Parvula placed her fan to her train.

" Let her lash it! " she said. " In this glorious room one is quite content to wait."

And indeed there could not be the least doubt that the drawing-room at Hare-Hatch House was sufficiently uplifting to be alone in without becoming dull.

Here were the precious Holbeins—the finest extant —and the Ozias Humphry in its original oval frame, while prominent above the great Jacobean fireplace, with a row of lamps shining footlight-wise beneath it, was the youthful portrait of the present mistress from the hand of Ingres.

Garbed in Greek draperies, she was seen leaning her head against a harpsichord, whose carved support rose perpendicularly from end to end of the canvas like some flower-wreathed capital.

Less redoubtable perhaps were an infinity of Morlands, fresh and fragrant, in their oblong, cross-ribboned frames, a Longhi or two—a Piazza, a Punchinello in a little square, and a brilliant croquis signed *Carmontelle* of a Duchess trifling with a strawberry.

By a jaguar-skin couch far down the room an array of long-back chairs in the splendid upholstery of the seventeenth century suggested to Lady Parvula's mind an occasional " public " correction. And everywhere ranged fortuitously about were *faïence* flower-tubs bearing large-leaved plants that formed tall canopies to the white, pensive statues grouped patiently beneath.

She was just passing a furtive hand over the promising

feet and legs of a Discobolus, broken off, unfortunately, at the height of the loins, as Mrs. Thoroughfare entered.

All billowing silks and defenceless embroideries, she was looking to-night like a good-natured sphinx —her rather bulging, etiolated cheeks and vivid scarlet mouth expanded in a smile.

" I know of no joy," she airily began, " greater than a cool white dress after the sweetness of confession."

Lady Parvula cast an evasive eye towards the supine form of a bronze hermaphrodite, whose long, tip-tilted, inquisitive nose protruded snugly above a smart Renaissance quilt.

" No! Really! Elizabeth! " she exclaimed.

Mrs. Thoroughfare breathed in a way that might have been called a sigh.

" And where is Gilda? " she asked.

" Gilda . . . Gilda's still at school! "

" Oh! "

" And Dick? "

" Dick . . . Dick's still at sea! "

" Wicked fellow."

"A crate of some wonderful etherised flowers," Mrs. Thoroughfare informed, pivoting with hands outspread, about a tripod surmounted by a small braziero, " came from him only this afternoon, from Ceylon."

Lady Parvula plied her fan.

" Even at Oomanton," she murmured, " certain of the new hybrids this year are quite too perfect."

" Eulalia and I often speak of the wondrous orchids at Oomanton Towers."

Lady Parvula expanded.

" We're very proud of a rose-lipped one," she said, " with a lilac beard."

" A lilac . . . *what?* " It was Mrs. Hurstpierpoint's voice at the door.

28

" Eulalia! "

" Is it Sodom? " she inquired in her gruff, commanding way, coming forward into the room.

She had a loose, shapeless gown of hectically-contrasted colours—one of Zenobia Zooker's hardiest inspirations—draped from the head à l'Évangile.

Lady Parvula tittered.

" Goodness, no," she said.

" Because Father Mahoney won't hear of it ever *before* dessert."

" How right."

" He seems to think it quite soon enough," the mistress of Hare murmured, passing an intimate arm about her old friend's waist.

Lady Parvula cooed half-fluttered. In a time-corroded mirror she could see herself very frail, and small, and piquant in its silver-sheeted depth.

" To be continually beautiful, like *you*, dear," her hostess said. " How I wish I could. . . ."

" Yet I date my old age," Lady Parvula replied, " from the day I took the lift first at the Uffizi! "

" You dear angel."

" One's envious, almost, of these country clowns, who live, and live, and live, and look so well! "

" Many find the climate here trying to begin with," Mrs. Hurstpierpoint said, " owing to the amount of cosmic activity there is; but the longevity of the Valmouthers attracts all kinds of visitors to the town."

" At the Strangers' a Contessa di Torre Nuevas has the room next to me—and *oh!* how she snores! "

" Do they make you comfortable? "

" Most."

" You must miss the society of your girl."

" Dear child. She is training under Luboff Baltzer —in Milan."

" To what end? "

" Music. And she is in such cruel despair. She says

Luboff insists on endless counterpoint, and *she* only wants to play valses! "

" She hardly sounds to be ambitious."

" It depends; measured by Scriabin's *Quasi-Valse*, or the *Valse in A flat major*, she may have quite intricate idylls. . . ."

Mrs. Thoroughfare simmered. " I do so love his *Étrangeté*," she said.

" Was it you, Betty," Mrs. Hurstpierpoint demanded, " before Office I heard amusing yourself in Our Lady? "

" I am sure, Eulalia, I forget."

Lady Parvula's hand wandered vaguely towards the laurel-leaf fillet that encompassed irresponsibly her pale, liver-tinted hair.

" After the Sixtine Chapel," she remarked, " I somehow think your Nuestra Señora de la Pena is the one I prefer."

" You *dear* you! You should have been with us Easter Day! Our little basilica was a veritable bower of love."

" Have you any more new relics? "

" Only the tooth of St. Automona Meris, for which," Mrs. Hurstpierpoint, in confidence, was moved to add, " I've had my tiara-stones turned into a reliquary."

" You funny animal! "

" If we go on as we go on," Mrs. Thoroughfare commented as dinner was ceremoniously announced, " we'll be almost *too* ornate! "

It was what they, each in their way, were ready for.

" I adore dining *en petit comité*," Lady Parvula exclaimed, accepting gaily her hostess's propellent arm.

It was past blue, uncurtained windows to the dining-room, that remained, too, uncurtained to the night.

In the taper-lit, perhaps pre-sixteenth-century room —a piece of *Laughing and Triumphing* needlework in the style of Rubens completely hid the walls—the capacious oval of the dinner-table, crowned by a monteith bowl filled with slipper-orchids, showed agreeably enough.

"Where can Father be?" Mrs. Hurstpierpoint wondered, sinking to her chair with a slight grimace. Rumour had it that she wore a bag of holly-leaves pinned to the lining of her every gown; it even asserted that she sometimes assumed spiked garters.

"He went to the carpenter's shop, Eulalia," Mrs. Thoroughfare replied, "to give 'a tap or two,' as he said, to your new *prie-dieu*."

"And so you've lost Père Ernest," Lady Parvula murmured, humbling a mitred napkin with a dreamy hand.

"Alas! our stationariness soon bored him. He preferred flitting about the world like you."

"I go about," Lady Parvula admitted, "as other fools, in quest of pleasure, and I usually find tedium."

"If I recollect," Mrs. Hurstpierpoint said, "the Valmouth cattle-show was *our* last gaiety."

"Your pathetic-eyed, curious oxen . . . it's a breed you don't see everywhere! My husband—my Haree-ee-ee" (either from coquetry or from some slight difficulty she experienced in pronouncing her y's, Lady Parvula pronounced "Harry" long) "tried them, in the park down at Oomanton Towers; but they didn't do."

"No?"

"They got leaner and leaner and leaner and leaner in spite of cakes and cakes and cakes and cakes. . . . Poor Haree-ee-ee, my dearly beloved lord, even allowed them on to the lawn, where they used to look in at the ground-floor windows. One dreadful evening —we were taking tea—a great crimson head and two huge horns tossed the cup I was holding out of my hands, which sent me off—I'm just all over nerves! —into a state of *défaillance;* the last thing you may imagine I wanted, as it was Gilda's last night at home."

31

" You should consult local advice."

" It's what I intend doing."

" We hear of several of our hidalgos having been immortalised lately, thanks to Victor Vatt."

Mrs. Thoroughfare smiled indulgently.

" Those disciples of his," she demurely said, " oh; are they all they seem? "

" Lady Lucy Saunter swears not! "

" Is Lady Lucy at Valmouth? "

" Indeed she is. . . . And *so* poorly and *so* run-down. She says her blood is nothing but rose-water."

" I suppose the town is full of imaginary invalids *comme toujours?* "

" My dear, one sees nothing else. So many horrid parliament-men come here apparently purely to bask."

Mrs. Thoroughfare's face lit.

" Like our two whips! " she made chucklingly rejoinder. " Last Epiphany in a fit of contrition we sent a tiny *enfant du chœur* (a dangerous, half-witted child . . . but pious: pious . . .! And with the sweetest face; oh hadn't Charlie a witching face last Epiphany, Eulalia? His hair's good yet, and so are his taper hands, but his voice has gone, and so too have his beautiful roses) into town for a couple of whips. They duly appeared. But two such old vote-hunters. . . . ' My God,' Eulalia said, ' we asked for whips and Thou sendest *scourges.*' "

" Well! Quite a harum-scarum, one of the Vile-islands, sits for Oomanton, who pretends, I believe," Lady Parvula breathed, " to be an advocate for Gilda; but if *I* ever venture to propose an alliance to my ewe-lamb usually she answers: 'I don't want to marry *any*-one, thank you, mama! I prefer to be free.' She has no real cognisance, dear lambkin, of anything at all."

" Sooner or later she'll make her choice! "

" Men, men! . . . ' They are always there,' dear, aren't they, as the Russians say? "

Mrs. Hurstpierpoint repressed a grimace.

"Nowadays," she murmured, "a man ... to me ... somehow ... oh! he is something so wildly *strange*."

"Strange?"

"Unglimpsable."

"Still, some men are ultra-womanly, and they're the kind I love!" Mrs. Thoroughfare chirruped.

"I suppose that none but those whose courage is unquestionable can venture to be effeminate?" Lady Parvula said, plunging a two-pronged fork into a "made" dish of sugared-violets served in aspic.

"It may be so."

"It was only in war-time, was it, that the Spartans were accustomed to put on perfumes, or to crimp their beards?"

"My dear, how your mind seems to dwell upon beards."

"Upon *beards?*"

"It's perfectly disgusting."

"In the old days do you remember ' Twirly ' Rogers?"

"Out with the Valmouth Drag," Mrs. Thoroughfare sighed, "how well he looked in his pink coat!"

Lady Parvula assented.

"Those meets," she said, "on the wintry cliffs above the world had a charm about them. One could count more alluring faces out with the Valmouth, my husband used to say, than with any other pack. The Baroness Elsassar—I can see her now on her great mauve mount with her profile of royalty in misfortune—never missed. Neither, bustless, hipless, chinless, did ' Miss Bligh '! It was she who so sweetly hoisted me to my saddle when I'd slid a-heap after the run of a ' fairy ' fox. We'd whiffed it—the baying of the dogs is something I shall never forget; dogs always know!—in a swede-field below your house from where it took us by break-neck, rapid stages—

(oh! oh!)—to the sands. There, it hurried off along the sea's edge, with the harriers in full cry; all at once, near Pizon Point, it vanished. Mr. Rogers, who was a little ahead, drew his horse in with the queerest gape —like a lost huntsman (precisely) in the *Bibliothèque bleue*."

" It's a wonder he didn't vomit."

" I and Miss Bligh lay on the beach for hours——!"

" With a *dominus vobiscum*," Mrs. Hurstpierpoint remarked, turning her head at the silken swish of her chaplain's gown.

Flecked with wood shavings, Saint Joseph-wise, it brought with it suggestions of Eastern men in intriguing, long burnooses; of sandalled feet; of shadûf singing boys; of creaking water-wheels and lucerne-laden camels.

Bowing her face before the stiff, proud thumb and crooked forefinger raised to bless, Mrs. Hurstpierpoint remained a moment as if in transport, looking, with her figured veils and fuzzed hair-wreathings, like some Byzantine peacock searching for fleas.

" Lulu Veuve? Veaujolais? Clos Voukay? Or Château-Thierry? " the butler broke the silence.

Lady Parvula hesitated.

" If only not to be too like everyone else, *mon ami*," she murmured, her perfervid, soul-tossed eyes wandering towards the priest, " you shall give me some of each."

Father Colley-Mahoney launched a dry, defensive cough, involuntarily starting Nit.

" How incomparable their livery is! " Lady Parvula commented.

" It has a seminary touch about it," Mrs. Hurstpierpoint conceded, " though at Head-quarters it's regarded (I fear!) as inclining to modernism, somewhat."

" Pray what's that? "

34

" Modernism? Ask any bishop."

Lady Parvula rippled.

" I once," she said (resolutely refusing a stirring salmis of cocks'-combs *saignant* with *Béchamel* sauce), " I once peeped under a bishop's apron! "

" Oh . . .? "

" And what ever did you see? " Mrs. Thoroughfare breathlessly asked.

" Well . . . I saw," Lady Parvula replied (helping herself to a few *pointes d'asperges à la Laura Leslie*), " I saw . . . the dear Bishop! "

Father Mahoney kindled.

" Apropos," he said, " his Eminence writes he is offering an ex-voto to Nuestra Señora of a silver heart."

" In any particular intention? "

" No. Its consecration he leaves to our discretion."

" He owes, they say," Mrs. Thoroughfare murmured, consulting the menu with Spanish gravity, " to women at least the half of his red hat. . . ."

Lady Parvula's glance explored the garden.

A hyacinthine darkness flooded the titanic cedars before the house above whose immemorial crests like a sad opal the moon was rising.

" Parvula," her hostess evinced concern, " you're tasting nothing."

" I shall wait," Lady Parvula made answer, " Eulalia, for the *Madeleines en surprise!* "

" An abbess, and one of my earliest penitents," Father Mahoney said, " professed to find ' delicious ' small slips of paper traced thickly across with holy texts."

" Really? . . . It sounds like parlour games! "

Mrs. Hurstpierpoint was moved to sigh.

" No one remembers cribbage now," she lamented, " or gleek, or bi-ri-bi."

" No; or ombre. . . ."

" Or lansquenet. . . ."

35

" Or spadille. . . ."

" Or brelan. . . ."

" But for cards, country evenings would be too slow! "

" Indeed, when Father reads us Johnny Bunyan after dinner I fall asleep," Mrs. Thoroughfare declared.

" Have you nothing brighter than that? "

" We read here," Father Mahoney interpolated, " books only of a theological trend. Not that," he disconsolately added, " the library upstairs doesn't contain a certain amount of Rabelaisian literature, I regret to say."

" Rabelaisian, Father? " Mrs. Hurstpierpoint faintly shrieked.

" I don't choose, my child, to think of some of the ' works ' we harbour."

" Those Jacobean dramatists, and the French erotic works of the eighteenth century, of course, would be free . . . but Père Ernest didn't reject them; many a stern metaphor have I heard him draw from *Dr. James's Powders* and *Mr. Foote's Tea*—and all the rest of it."

Lady Parvula considered with a supercilious air the immaterial green of a lettuce-leaf.

" Oh, well," she said, " even at Oomanton, I dare say, there are some bad books too; in fact, I know there are! Once my ewe-lamb came to me with what appeared to be a mediæval lutrin. ' Oh, mama,' she said, ' I've found such a funny word.' ' What is it, my precious? ' I said. ' ——, mama! ' she answered with the most innocent lips in life . . . which sent me off —I'm just all over nerves!—into a fainting state; fairly scaring my lambkin out of her wits."

Mrs. Hurstpierpoint extended towards her guest a hand that was not (as Lady Parvula confided afterwards to the Lady Lucy Saunter) too scrupulously clean.

" Those fainting-fits," she said, motioning an order

to Nit as he flitted by with an ingenuity of tartelettes, "should be taken in time. For my sake, allow Dr. Dee of Valmouth to systematically overhaul you."

" Overhaul me! What for? "

But Mrs. Thoroughfare uttered a cry.

" Oh poor wee mothlet! " she exclaimed, leaning forward to extricate a pale-winged moth, struggling tragically in one of the sconces of a candelabra. . . .

" If ffines to-night was not enough to infuriate an archangel! " Mrs. Hurstpierpoint commented, resplendently trailing (the last toothsome dish having been served) towards the holy-water stoup of old silver-work behind the door.

Lady Parvula joined her.

"After your superexcellent champagne," she exclaimed, " I feel one ought to go with bared feet in pilgrimage to Nuestra Señora and kindle a wax light or two."

" My dear, I believe you've latent proclivities! "

" Eulalia! "

" Parvula! "

" Never."

" Ah, don't say that."

" Dearest," Lady Parvula perversely marvelled, " what a matchless lace berthe! "

" It was part of my corbeille——"

" Like *doubting Thomas*, I must touch with my hands."

" Touch! Touch! "

Father Mahoney fidgeted.

" Beyond the vigil-lamp," he objected, " Nuestra Señora will be quite obscure."

" Then all the more reason, Father, to illumine it!" Lady Parvula reasoned.

" Are you resolved, Parvula? "

" Of course. And I'm agog to see the tooth, too, of St. Automona Meris (Do you imagine she ever really ate with it horrid Castilian garlic *olla cocida?* Or

37

purple *pistos insalada?* She, and Teresa together, in some white *posada*, perhaps, journeying South), and your Ghirlandajo and the miracle-working effigy, and afterwards, until the fly comes round, you shall teach me gleek! ''

" You dear angel . . . it's very simple! "

" Then let us play for modest points."

Mrs. Hurstpierpoint crossed herself with her fan.

" As if," she horror-struck said, " I should consent to play for immodest ones! Are you coming Elizabeth, too? " she asked.

" In one moment, Eulalia; I must speak to Father first," Mrs. Thoroughfare replied, folding her arms lightly across the back of her chair.

" Don't, dear, desert us! " Mrs. Hurstpierpoint, withdrawing, enjoined.

There was a short pent silence.

" Do you think, Father," Mrs. Thoroughfare broke it at last, " she suspects? "

" Rest assured, my poor child," Father Mahoney answered, " your confession to me to-night exceeds belief."

" Was there ever such a quandary! " Mrs. Thoroughfare jabbered.

" They obeyed the surge of their blood—what else? " Father Mahoney dispassionately said.

Mrs. Thoroughfare's full cheeks quivered.

"Oh, my darling boy," she burst out, "how *could* you!"

" My poor child, try not to fret."

" It makes one belch, Father—belch."

" They're joined irremediably, I understand? "

" From what he writes I conclude the worst."

" Won't you show me what he says? "

" The card," she murmured, drawing it from her dress, " is covered, I fear, by the chemicals that were in the crate, gummed to the stem as it was of a nauseating lily."

38

" Decipher the thing, then, to me—if you will."

Mrs. Thoroughfare adjusted a lorgnon tearfully to her nose.

" ' These are the native wild-flowers,' he writes (what, I wonder, Father, must the others be!), ' the native wild-flowers of my betrothed bride's country. Forgive us, and bless us, mother. Ten thousand loves to you all.' "

" O, wretched boy."

" O, Father."

" That ever any Black woman should perform the honours at Hare! "

Mrs. Thoroughfare smiled mirthlessly.

" Well—if it comes to that—Eulalia, *herself*, to-night, is more than grubby," she said.

V

THE installation of a negress at the " Nook," Mrs.
Yajñavalkya's old-style dwelling in the Market Square,
came to Valmouth, generally, as a surprise.

Almost from the outset of her arrival in the town,
soft-muted music, the strange, heart-rending, mournful music of the East—suggestive of apes, and pearls,
and bhang, and the colour blue—was to be heard,
surging from the Nook in monotonous improvisa-
tion.

Madame Mimosa, the demi-mondaine, the only
" one " there was thereabouts, hearing it from the
Villa Concha, next door, fancied she detected rivalry,
competition—*the younger generation*—and took to her
bravura (cerise chiffon, and a long, thick, black aigrette)
before the clock told noon. Nurse Yates, hard by,
heard " zithers " too, and flattered herself the time
was ripe to oust Mrs. Yajñavalkya from the town,
"automatically" capturing her clients as they dropped
away. Mrs. Q. Comedy, *née* Le Giddy, ever alert to
flare an auction, told her Quentin she supposed Mrs.
Yajñavalkya would shortly be giving up her house
and going off into Valopolis, or New-Valmouth,
where she might conduct a *bagnio* with more facility,
perhaps, than beneath the steeple of the church. While
all the time, shining smiles, Mrs. Yajñavalkya herself
went about affairs much in her usual way.

Of a morning early she would leave the Nook
followed by a little whey-faced English maid, to whom
she allowed twelve pounds a year " because she is so
white," to take her way towards the provision stalls
encamped beneath John Baptist Daleman's virile, but

rudimentary, statue in the square, where, flitting from light to shade, she would exchange perhaps a silver coin against a silver fish, or warm-leafed cauliflower, half dead on the market stones. Sometimes, quickly dismissing her little Gretchen, she would toddle off up Peace Street into Main Street, and enter, without knocking, the house of Dr. Dee, but more frequently mistress and maid would return to the Nook together, when almost immediately from her chimneys would be seen to rise a copious torrent of smoke.

From the Strangers' Hotel across the way Lady Parvula de Panzoust, like the local residents themselves, had been a puzzled spectator of the small particular coterie at the Nook, since, to her ever-deepening vexation, her shepherd-with-the-dog was a constant caller there.

. Had he anything, then, the matter? His constitution, was it not the mighty thing it seemed? His agile figure (glowing through corduroys and hob-nailed boots; his *style d'amour*), was it nothing but a sham? Or had he an intrigue, perhaps, with one or other of the women of the house?

Now and then a dark face framed in unbound hair would look out through a turret window of the Nook, as if moved to home-sickness at the cries of a beautiful cockatoo that hung all day in the window of Sir Victor Vatt's sitting-room at the hotel.

" Dear Vatt," the bird would say with sonorous inflections, taking off some artist, or sitter perhaps, " dear Vatt! He is splendid; so o-ri-gi-nal and exuberant; like an Italian Decorator." Or, *vivo:* " Now, Vatt! Do me a Poussin." Or, the inflection changing *languido dolce:* " Come, Vatt! Paint me in a greenhouse . . . in a st-oove; a little exotic; paint me (my little Victor!) like Madame Cézanne! They say," *meno languido,* " they say he gave her one hundred and fifteen sittings! Pretty Poll! "

Loiterers in the Market Square, observing the attentive negress trim the window, smiled and called her a caution, more cautious-like, said they in the local vernacular, than " Old Mrs. Rub-me-down," inferring Mrs. Yajñavalkya. Lady Parvula de Panzoust, alone, a sure connoisseur of all amative values, was disposed to allow the negress her dues, divining those ethnologic differences, those uneasy nothings, that again and again in the history of the world have tempted mankind to err. She descried, therefore, whenever the parrot's loquaciousness induced the negress to look out, a moon-faced girl with high-set, scornful eyes almost in her forehead and bow-curved pagan lips of the colour of rose-mauve stock. Her anatomy, singularly independent in every way, was, Lady Parvula surmised, that of a little *woman* of twelve. Was it, she asked herself, on this black Venus' account Adonis visited the Nook? Or was it for other reasons, graver, sadder ones . . . such as, for instance, dressing the gruesome injury of the boar?

One sunny May-day morning, full of unrest, Lady Parvula de Panzoust left the hotel for a turn on the Promenade. It was a morning of pure delight. Great clouds, breaking into dream, swept slowly across the sky, rolling down from the uplands behind Hare-Hatch House, above whose crumbling pleasances one single sable streak, in the guise of a coal-black negress, prognosticated rain.

" Life would be perfect," she mused, " if only I hadn't a corn! " But the Oriental masseuse was the sole proficient of the chiropodist's art at Valmouth, and Lady Parvula de Panzoust felt disinclined to bare her tender foot to the negress's perspicacious gaze. Yet after going a few painful yards this is what she realised she must do. " After all," she reflected, " I may perhaps ascertain her pastoral client's condition, and so free my mind from doubt! "

42

She was looking charmingly matinal in a simple
tweed costume, with a shapely if perhaps *invocative* hat,
very curiously indented, and well cocked forward
above one ear. She held a long ivory-handled sunshade in the form of a triple-headed serpent, and a
book that bore the irreproachable Christian title
Embrassons Nous.

"And who knows," she sighed, lifting Mrs.
Yajñavalkya's sun-fired knocker with a troubled
hand, " he may even be there himself! "

The little chalk-faced maid that answered the door
said her mistress was in, and preceding the evident
"London lady" up a short flight of stairs, ushered
her with a smile of triumph into a small but crowded
cabinet whose windows faced the Square.

" Is it for a douche, m'm," she asked, " or ought I
to start the steam? "

" Not on *my* account! " Lady Parvula murmured
with dilated retinas, scanning the signed diplomas and
framed credentials displayed upon the walls. A coloured
"Insurance" almanac, privately marked with initials
and crosses—engagements no doubt of Mrs. Yajñavalkya's—gladdened gaily their midst.

" Chance me finding her," she reflected, moving
involuntarily towards a brilliant draped mirror above
the chimney-place, where a tall piece of branched coral
was stretched up half-forbiddingly against the glass.

Through its pink sticks she could see reflected in
the room behind part of a calico-covered couch with
the negress's bureau beyond, on which at present stood
a half-eaten orange and a jar of white pinks.

A twitter of negro voices was shrilly audible through
the wood partition of the wall.

" *Yahya!* "

" *Wazi jahm?* "

" *Ah didadidacti, didadidacti.*"

" *Kataka mukha?* "

" *Ah mawardi, mawardi.* "

" *Jelly.* "

" A breeze about their jelly! " Lady Parvula conjectured, complacently drawing nearer the window.

Before the Villa Concha, a little curtained carriage attached to an undocked colt with a bell at its ear signified that Madame Mimosa was contemplating shortly a drive.

Through what blue glebe or colza-planted plains would her rainbow axles turn?

Mrs. Yajñavalkya's ambling step disturbed her speculations.

" Have I not de satisfaction, " she ubiquitously began, " ob addressing Milady Panzoust? "

Lady Parvula nodded.

" I believe you do chiropody? " she said.

" Dat is a speciality ob de house—de cultivation ob de toes. Vot is dair so important? O wen I consider de foot . . . de precious precious foot! For de foot support de body; it bear de burden ob ten thousand treasures! . . . *Kra.* And dat's vot I alvays say. "

" Undoubtedly, " Lady Parvula assented, " whatever there *is*, it bears. "

" It gib gentle rise to ebberything, " Mrs. Yajñavalkya pursued.

" Perhaps—sometimes—it carries charms. "

" *Ukka-kukka!* " the negress broke off, dropping darkly to the floor. " My niece, Niri-Esther, she fill de flower vases so full dat de water do all drip down and *ro-vine* de carpet. "

" Then of course she's in love? "

" Niri-Esther! "

" Now and then an interesting patient must wish to approach you. "

" I alvays, " Mrs. Yajñavalkya blandly yapped, " decline a gentleman. Often ze old greybeards zey say, ' Oh, Mrs. Yaj,' zey say, ' include our sex.' And

44

I laugh and I say, 'I've enough to do wif my own!'"

Lady Parvula surrendered smilingly her shoes.

"Still, I sometimes see," she said, "call here a young tall man with his dog."

"He call only to fetch de fowls dat flit across to my acacia-tree from de farm."

"Is that all?"

"Being so near de church, de house is open to ebbery passing ghoul. De incubes and de succubes dat come in, and are so apt to molest . . . ob an evening especially, ven de sun fall and de sky turn all caprice, I will constantly dispatch my little maid to beg, to implore, and to beseech dat Dairyman Tooke will remove his roosters."

"Dairyman Tooke?"

"Or his prize sow, maybe—a sow! Ah, dat is my abomination!"

"Probably the antipathy springs through the belief in reincarnation."

"No doubt at all dat is one ob de causes."

"The doctrine of Transubstantiation must often tell on your nerves."

"When I die," Mrs. Yajñavalkya said, her eyes disappearing expiringly in their sockets, "I would not wish to be transubstantiated into a horse or a cow or a sheep or a cat. No; oh no! I will wish to be changed into a little bird, wid white, white feathers; treasuring," she wistfully added, "meantime de poet's words:

"'My mother bore me in the southern wild,
  And I am black, but O! my soul is white.'"

"Your songsters too," Lady Parvula said, "have also their poignance."

"Ah! when Niri-Esther read Tagore," Mrs. Yajñavalkya glowed, "dat is something beautiful! Dat is something to make de tears descend."

45

" To hear her render the love lyrics of her country, just the most typical things, would interest me immensely if it might some day be arranged."

" But why not? "

" A *séance* in your garden amidst the acacia leaves— Mademoiselle Esther and I! And when the young man came to retrieve his birds, I vow he'd find no turkey!"

" Believe me," Mrs. Yajñavalkya murmured, indrawing succulently her cheeks and circumspectly toying with her file, " believe me, he's awfully choice."

" He has youth."

" He's awfully, awfully choice! " the negress murmured, admiring the intricate nerve-play of her patient's foot.

" It's just a Valmouth type," Lady Parvula observed.

" Ah! It is more dan dat."

" How? "

" Much more in ebbery way." Mrs. Yajñavalkya looked insoluble.

" I don't I fear follow . . ." Lady Parvula gasped.

" I have known what love is, I! " The negress heaved. " Dair are often days ven I can neither eat, nor drink, nor sleep, ven my fingers hab no strength at all (massage den is quite impossible)—I am able only to groan and groan and groan—ah, my darling!"

" A nigger? "

" A nigger! No. He was a little blonde Londoner —all buttoned-and-braided, one ob de *chasseurs* at your hotel."

" Thank you." Lady Parvula looked detached.

" De dear toe," the operatress raised a glinting, sooty face, " is quite inflamed! De skin," with unwitting cynicism she theorised, " may vary, but de Creator ob de universe has cast us all in de same mould; and dat's vot I alvays say."

" In what part, tell me, is your home? "

" Here! " the negress lisped.

" Geographically, I mean."

" Geographically, we're all so scattered. Von ob my brother, Djali, he in Ujiji Land. *Kra.* He a Banana-Inspector. Official. He select de virgin combs from off de tree; dat his Pash-on, dat his Cult. Other brother, Boujaja, he in Taihaiti. He a lady-killer, well-to-do-ish; he three wives, *kra;* and dose three women are my sisters-in-law. . . . De Inspector, he no marry; I don't know why! "

" Then your niece," Lady Parvula pressed, " is from Taihaiti? "

But Mrs. Yajñavalkya was abstruse.

" Do you care to undergo a course ob me? " she asked. " For de full course—I make you easy terms; and I alvays try," she airily cozened, " to end off wid a charming sensation."

" Massage merely as sensation does not appeal to me:—and otherwise, thank you, I'm perfectly well."

" I gib a massage lately to de widowed Duchess ob Valmouth for less! Yajñavalkya, she laugh and say after I had applied my court cream (half a crown; five shillings): 'Yajñavalkya, your verve, it's infectious.' ' My what, your grace?' I say. 'Your verve,' she reply; 'it's so *catching.*' "

" I always admired her," Lady Parvula remarked, " you'd almost say she was a man."

" Her testimonial is on my bureau dair."

" You must be proud of your tributes."

" Zey come from all sides. . . . Queen Quattah, she write again and again for my balsam ob mint, or my elixir ob prunes; but my greatest discovery, milady, my dear, was de use ob tiger-lily pollen for ' superfluous hair.' "

Lady Parvula moved uncomfortably in her chair. She was sufficiently alert to feel the animal magnetism from a persistent pair of eyes.

" *Wushi!* " Mrs. Yajñavalkya turned too.

47

" *Kataka?* " a voice came from the door.

" My relative Niri-Esther," Mrs. Yajñavalkya explained, " she ask me what I do."

" She seems," Lady Parvula commented, " to have been crying."

" She cry for a sting ob a wasp dat settle on her exposed bosom. I tell her—at de window—she shouldn't expose it! "

" Oh? "

" De wasps dis year dey are a plague."

" *Kataka . . .; kataka mukha?* "

Advancing with undulating hesitation, the young black girl brought with her a something of uttermost strangeness into the room.

Incontestably, she was of a superior caste to Mrs. Yajñavalkya, albeit her unorthodox values tended, perhaps, to obscure a little her fundamental merit.

She wore a dishabille of mignonette-green silk and a bead-diapered head-dress that added several inches to her height; her finger-slim ankles were stained with lac and there were rings of collyrium about her eyes.

With one hand clasped in the other behind her back, she stood considering Lady Parvula de Panzoust.

" *Chook,*" Mrs. Yajñavalkya grumbled.

" *Owesta wan?* "

" *Obaida.* "

" She has the exuberance of an orchid," Lady Parvula cried. " Could Sfax—he is my gardener down at Oomanton Towers—behold her now, he'd exclaim, ' A Urania Alexis, your ladyship! ' and pop her into a pot."

" Niri-Esther's clothes, I sometimes venture to tink, are a little too vainglorious! ! ! At her age," Mrs. Yajñavalkya retailed, " and until I was past eighteen, I nebber had more in de course ob a year dan a bit ob cotton loincloth. You may wear it how you please, my poor mother would say, but dat is all

48

you'll get! And so, dear me, I generally used to put it on my head."

" She eyes one like a cannibal."

" Are you quite well? " the young black woman waveringly asked.

Lady Parvula answered with a nod.

" Come here and show me," she said.

" I drop de *mushrabiyas*—; so nobody den can see in!"

" Why O, why O," Mrs. Yajñavalkya complained, "will dat *hetæra's* horrid coachman draw up alvays juſt opposite to my gate? "

" She is later dan usual to-day," her relative re-joined.

" Wears her horse," the elder negress demanded, " a rose? "

" De poor unhappy thing; he wear both a favour and a ſtrap."

" The looser the miſtress . . . the tighter the bear-ing-rein! " Lady Parvula remarked.

Mrs. Yajñavalkya languished.

" She dribe her cheſtnut for day work, and reserbe a white for evening use. Not dat," she amplified, " one move more rapidly dan de other; no, oh no; Madame Mimosa refuse to dribe her horses fleet! She seldom elect to aribe betimes; she say it ' good ' to keep de clients waiting. It's a queſtion ob policy wif her dat ' two hours late.' "

" I suppose simply to engender suspense."

" *C'eſt une femme qui sait enrager. Allez!* "

" You know French? "

" Like ebberything else! "

Lady Parvula expanded.

" I said to my maid this morning: ' Oh, Louison!' I said, ' what does the prommy place here remind you of? ' ' Of nothing, your ladyship,' replied she. ' Oh, *doesn't* it? ' I said; ' well, it does me! It reminds me of the Promenade des Sept Heures at Spa.' "

49

" Ah, de dear spot! "

" For brio, and for beauty and from the look of the trees, I said to her, it reminds me of the Promenade des Sept Heures at Spa."

" You may go far before you will find a prettier place dan dis is."

" True, I never go out but I see someone sketching."

Mrs. Yajñavalkya was convulsed.

" A certain Valmouth widow, living yon side de church, found a Francis Fisher lately lying in her ditch (some small *plein-air* ob his, I suppose, he had thrown away), so she forwarded it to London just to ask what it would fetch, and sold it to a dealer for more dan fifty pounds."

" Bravo. I must try to pick up a Vatt! "

" Curious how he faber de clodhopper type. Who would want to hang a beggar on his walls? Dair are enough in de world without. Believe me."

" Indeed there are."

" An artist I alvays admire, now," the negress murmured, retying with coquetry her patient's shoe-string, " is Mr. FitzGeorge! All his models are ladies . . . daughters ob clergymen, 'daughters of colonels . . . and even his male sitters are," she twittered, " sons ob good houses."

" Some one should paint your niece!" Lady Parvula rose remarking.

" *Fanoui ah maha?* "

" *Tauroua ta.* "

" *Yahya.* "

" What's that she says? "

" That she will be glad to make music for you at any time."

" That will be delightful."

" And I, also," the dark-skinned woman assumed her silkiest voice, " will endeavour to have a few fugitive fowls over from de farm. De dogs shall bark, and de birds shall fly (de sky is full ob de whirring ob wings), but de lover and his beloved shall attain Nirvana."

" Nirvana? "

" Leave it to me and you and he shall come to gether."

" Oh, impossible."

" Leave it to me."

" I never run *any* risks," Lady Parvula babbled.

" Risks! Vot risks? Risks! . . . O Allah la Ilaha! Shall I tell you vot de Yajñavalkya device is? Vot it has been dis thousand and thousand ob year? It is *bjopti. Bjopti!* And vot does *bjopti* mean? It means *discretion. S-s-s-s-s-s-s-s-s-s-s-s-s-s-s-s-s-s-s-s-s-s-s-sh!*"

Lady Parvula toyed reflectively with her rings.

" At balls in a quilted skirt and with diamonds in my hair I've often been hugely admired as a shepherdess," she said. " I well remember," she tittered, " the success I had one evening—it was at the British Embassy in Paris—as a shepherdess of Lely. I had a lamb (poor, innocent darling, but so heavy and so hot; worse than any child) with me, that sprang from my arms quite suddenly while I was using my powder-puff and darted bleating away beneath the legs of Lord Clanlubber (at that time ambassador) out into the Champs Élysées, where it made off, I afterwards heard, towards the Etoile. And *I* never saw it again! So that you see," she murmured, depositing her benefactress's fee vaguely upon the couch. "I've a strong bond with shepherds, having myself, once, lost a lamb. . . ."

" In a like rig-up you would stir de soul ob Krishna, as de milkmaid Rádhá did! "

" I'm quite content to ' stir ' my neighbour instead."

" Believe me," the dark-skinned woman murmured, following her visitor to the stairhead, with sigh that shook the house, " he's awfully, awfully choice! "

" ____ . . ."

" He has a wee mole—on de forehead! "

" Ah, and he has another: yes! in the deep pool above his upper-lip—; the channel affair. . . ."

" He's *awfully* choice! "

" *C'est un assez beau garçon,*" Lady Parvula answered with a backward æsthetic glance.

Leaning from the hand-rail, like some adoring chimpanzee, Mrs. Yajñavalkya watched her recede, the wondrous crown of the vanishing hat suggesting forcibly the peculiar attributes of her own tribal gods.

The shadow upon the forewall of her little English maid descending the staircase with a chamber-pot from above recalled her to herself.

"Ah, *zoubé kareen pbf!* Why weren't you in readiness, Carry, to open de door? " she inquired, returning thoughtfully towards her sanctum with the intent to sterilise her tools.

On a spread kerchief, pitcher-posture, upon the floor her relative was bleaching idly her teeth with a worn bit of bone, while turning round and round like a water-wheel in her henna-smeared fingers the glass hoop-clasp at her abdomen.

Mrs. Yajñavalkya gave way to a joyous chuckle.

" Mrs. Richard Thoroughfare, Mrs. Richard Thoroughfare! " she addressed the prostrate belle.

" *Chakrawaki—wa?* "

" Mrs. Dick, Mrs. Thorough-dick, Mrs. Niri fairy!"

" *Suwhee?* "

With an eloquent listening eye, Mrs. Yajñavalkya laid a hand to her ear.

" De bridal litter," she playfully announced, " from Hare-Hatch House, is already at de far corner ob de adjacent street! "

The water-wheel ceased as the mauve lips parted.

" Ah, Vishnu! " the young black girl yawned. " Vot den can make it come so slow? "

V I

A CAMPAIGN of summer storms of a quasi-tropical nature was delaying the hay harvest that in Valmouth, as in the neighbouring Garden Isles, was usually celebrated before the last week in May.

Not since the year 17—,when milord Castlebrilliant's curricle was whirled to sea with her ladyship within, had there been such vehement weather.

At Hare-Hatch House the finest hornbeam upon the lawn had succumbed, none too silently, while in the park several of the centennial cedars were fallen, giving to the grounds somehow a tragic, classic look.

And indeed, with her favourite hornbeam, Mrs. Hurstpierpoint's nerves had also given way.

One afternoon, just as the bell of Nuestra Señora was sounding Terce, the lament of the peacocks announced a return of the storm. Since mid-day their plangent, disquieting cries had foretold its approach. Moving rapidly to and fro in their agitation, their flowing fans sweeping rhythmically the ground, they traced fevered curves beneath the overarching trees, orchestrating, with barbarity, as they did so, their strident screech with the clangour of the chapel bell that seemed, as it rang, to attract towards it a bank of tawny gold, cognac-coloured cloud, ominously fusing to sable.

Sauntering up and down in the shadow of the chapel wing, the mistress of the manor, this afternoon, was also mingling her voice, intermittently, as though a plaintive, recurring motif in a slightly trying musical score, with her birds and her bell. " Eliza! Eliza! " she called.

53

Seated upon the fallen hornbeam, Mrs. Thorough-fare was regarding distraitly the sky.

Ever since the windy weather a large pink kite like a six-humped camel had made above the near wood its extraneous appearance. To whom, Mrs. Thoroughfare asked herself, bewildered, could such a monstrous toy belong? There was something about it that alarmed her, alarmed her more than all the storm-clouds put together.

" E'lizabeth! "

As if cleft by passing lightning the name on the tense hot air writhed lugubriously away amid the trees.

" In, in," Mrs. Thoroughfare beseeched.

But Mrs. Hurstpierpoint had already turned towards the house, where an under-footman was busily closing the ground-floor windows against the dark, shining spots of falling rain. And falling too, Mrs. Thorough-fare noted, came the bewildering kite, headforemost, as though jerked smartly earthward in the flyer's hand. A burst of near thunder sent her perforce to join her friend, whose finer, more delicate nature was ever apt to be affected by a storm.

She found her in a corner of the vast drawing-room clasping a " blessed " rosary while listening in a state of compressed hysterics to the storm.

" I'm an old woman now ": she was telling her beads: "and my only wish is to put my life in order— was that another flash? "

" Darling."

" Is that you, my little Lizzie? "

" Tchut! Eulalia."

" Oh-h-h-h! . . . Betty dear! The *awful* vividness of the lightning! " Mrs. Hurstpierpoint wailed.

Through the nine tall windows with their sun-warped, useless shutters, like violet-darting swallows, the lightning forked.

" Let us go," Mrs. Thoroughfare said in a slightly unsteady voice, " shall we both, and confess? "

" Confess! "

" Father's in Nuestra now."

" My dear, in my opinion, the lightning's so much more ghastly through the stained-glass windows! "

Mrs. Thoroughfare pressed her hands lightly to her admired associate's humid brow.

" Dear mother was the same," she cooed. " Whenever it thundered she'd creep away under her bed, and make the servants come and lie down on top . . . (it was in the eighteenth century of course . . .) so that should the brimstone burst it must vent its pristine powers on them. Poor innocent! It was during a terrific thunderstorm at Brighton, or *Brighthelmstone* as they called it then, that several of the domestics fell above her head. . . . And the fruits of that storm, as I believe I've told you before, Eulalia, are in the world to-day."

" My dear . . . every time the weather breaks you must needs hark back to it."

Mrs. Thoroughfare showed pique.

" Well *I*," she said, ambling undeterred towards the door, " intend to pray."

" Who knows but our prayers may meet? " Mrs. Hurstpierpoint murmured, returning to her beads, that in the sombre brilliance of the darkened room shed different pale and supernatural lights as they swung from side to side in her nerveless hands.

" Adorable Jesus," her mouth moved faintly beneath the charcoal shadow of her moustache, " love me even as I do Thee, and I," she deeply breathed, " will land Thee a fish! I will hook Thee a heretic; even though," her tongue passed wistfully over her lips, " to gain an open sinner I should be impelled to go to London, O Lord; for I will bend to Thy Sovereign Purpose (irrespective of my little kitchen-maid

55

whom I most certainly mean to force) a thorough-going infidel; something very putrid . . . very lost. And so, O my Saviour Dear," beatifically she raised her face, " I will make Thee retribution for the follies of my youth."

Her lips grew still.

From the adjacent chapel soft, insinuating voices assailed agreeably the ear.

" Victories . . ." " Vanquish . . ." " Virtue . . ." " Virgin . . ."

Mrs. Hurstpierpoint's veiled glance dropped from her rafters, hovering with a certain troubled diffidence over the ruff and spade-beard of a dashing male portrait, until it dwelt on the face of the time-piece on the commode below, so placed as to exclude as far as possible the noble arch of her kinsman's shapely legs. The slow beat of the flower-wreathed pendulum usually filled the room.

Long ago, it was related, it had been consulted in an hour of most singular stress. And it was as if still some tragic pollen of anguish-staring eyes clung to the large portentous numerals of the Louis-Sixteenth dial. Two steel key-holes in the white full face loomed now like beauty patches in the flickering light.

" I feel I'm ready for my tea," Mrs. Hurstpierpoint reflected, taking up an invalidish posture on the jaguar-skin couch.

The inebriating, slightly acrid perfume of a cobra lily, wilting in its vase, awoke solicitous thought within her of her distant heir.

Soon the dear lad would give up his junketings, she mused, and take to himself a wife.

Her eyes absorbed fondly the room.

" Ah! Ingres! " she sighed, " your portrait of me is still indeed most like . . . more like and much more pleasing, I think, than the marble Dalou did. . . ." And fearful lest she should fall a victim to her own seductiveness, against the peevish precepts of the church, she averted her eyes towards the young naval officer in the carved Renaissance frame, into whose gold-wrapped, slim-wristed hands, with the long and lissom fingers swelling towards their tips like big drop pearls, Hare-Hatch House and all its many treasures would one day pass.

A flare of dazzling brightness on the wainscoting caused her to knit her brows, and like a tall reed, wrapped in silk, her maid, wheeling a light chaufferette, advanced towards her.

" Is the worst of the storm yet over, Fowler, do you consider?" Mrs. Hurstpierpoint gently groaned.

The maid's sallow face, flame-lit, looked malign as she drooped her trim-coiffed head.

"Now that the wind has deprived the statues of their fig leaves, 'm," she replied, "I hardly can bear to look out."

" Oh? *Has* it? What? Again? "

" All round the courtyard and in the drive you'd think it was October from the way they lie! "

" Sister Ecclesia will be distressed going home, I fear. Even *an altar-cupid*—— She's so sensitive," Mrs. Hurstpierpoint remarked.

" It's mostly dark, 'm, before she's done."

" Unless the summer quickly mends the Hundred Club's fête must be postponed! "

" It's odd, 'm," the waiting woman answered, adding a pinch of incense to the fire, " how many a centenarian seems more proof against exposure than others not yet in their prime. Only a short while since my Lady Parvula's maid—she's been spending the day here among us—got caught in the wet while taking a turn with Miss Fencer and Nit; and now there she is, sitting before the kitchen range, in borrowed hose, with a glass of hot toddy."

" I dare say her licentious stories have brought on this storm! "

57

" She was very full to be sure at meal-time of a fraudulent marriage, saying how no one or nothing was inviolate or safe."

" The sole dependable marriage is the Spiritual marriage! On that alone can we implicitly rely."

" And she was very full, too, of her ladyship's jewelled pyjamas."

" Holy Virgin! "

" The storm sounds almost above us."

" Lift the lid of the long casket—and pick me a relic," Mrs. Hurstpierpoint enjoined, surveying apprehensively the dark clumps of wind-flogged trees upon the lawn.

" Any one in particular, 'm? " the maid inquired, slipping, with obedient alacrity, across the floor.

" No; but not a leg-bone, mind! A leg-bone relic somehow——" she broke off, searching with her great dead eye dreaming the sad camphor-hued hills for the crucifix and wayside oratory that surmounted the topmost peak.

" You used to say the toe, 'm, of the married sister of the Madonna, the one that was a restaurant proprietress (Look alive there with those devilled-kidneys, and what is keeping Fritz with that sweet-omelette?), in any fracas was particularly potent."

" Yes . . . bring the toe of the Madonna's married sister, and then come and read to me out of Père Pujol," her mistress answered, it being one of her chosen modes of penance (as well as a convenient means of paving the way to papalism) to call from time to time on her servants to come and read to her aloud. How often afterwards, in the soundless watches of the night, must the tonic words of a Pujol, or a brother Humphrey Caton, recur to dull procrastinating minds linked, made earthly in souvenir, with her own kind encouraging looks! Indeed, as a certain exalted churchman had excellently expressed it once, Oral-punishment, the mortification of the sparkling ear, was more delightful to heaven inasmuch as frequently it was more far-reaching than a knot in a birch or a nail in a boot.

But with Fowler, one of the earliest converts of the house, there was no need any more to push to extremes.

" *Figlia mia*," she jarringly began with a great thick " G " fully equal, her mistress reckoned, to a plenary indulgence alone, " *figlia mia*, examine your conscience, ask your heart, invoke that inner voice which always tells the truth, and never, no, never, betrays us! For the spark will live through the rains, lighting up dead fires: fire which is still fire, but with purer flame. . . ."

" Lest your cap-pin kindles, *presto* there. Never," Mrs. Hurstpierpoint intervened, " read of bad weather during storm! "

" One day St. Automona di Meris, seeing a young novice yawning, suddenly spat into her mouth, and *that* without malice or thought of mischief. Some ninety hours afterwards the said young novice brought into the world the Blessed St. Elizabeth Bathilde, who, by dint of skipping, changed her sex at the age of forty and became a man."

" A *man*—! Don't speak to me of *men*. Especially one of that description! " Mrs. Hurstpierpoint rapped. " Inflict something else."

" Something more poetical perhaps? "

" What is that thick, twine-coloured linen book I see the back of, beneath the young mistress's shawl? "

" Anthropology again, I expect, 'm," Fowler answered.

" This craze for anthropology with her is something altogether new."

" It frets her to form no idea of the tribes the Captain's been among."

" It only makes her dream. She was talking so

(being forced to fly to my little rosewood night-stool, I overheard her) in her sleep again."

"Miss Fencer was saying so, too. Only this morning (in calling her) she heard her say: 'I will *not* go in beads to the opera.' (Or was it 'berries' she said?) 'Tell King Mbmonbminbon so!' Anyway, Miss Fencer was so completely seized she just emptied the early tea vessel on to the floor."

Mrs. Hurstpierpoint exchanged with her maid a lingering, expressive glance.

"I *know* she's worried! I *know* she's keeping something from me! and I *know* she'll tell me in the end!" so the dependent, who was apt to read her mistress's face with greater accuracy than she did her books, interpreted the glance.

"The volume I find, 'm, beneath the shawl," she said, "is the *Tales from Casanova*."

"Child that my soul's treasure is!" There was a second significant glance.

"Well, well; for St. Francis's sake," Mrs. Hurstpierpoint said, steeling herself to listen, "an Italian story is always permitted at Hare."

"There was once upon a time two sisters," Fowler falteringly began, "named Manette and Marton, who lived with a widowed aunt, a certain Madame Orio, in the city of Venice. The disposition of these fair Venetians was such that——, such——," she floundered.

"Their disposition? . . . Yes? It was such?"

"Such——"

"That?"

". . . Well, I declare!"

"How often, Fowler," Mrs. Hurstpierpoint said with some asperity, "must I beg you not to employ that ridiculous phrase in my hearing?"

"Very good, 'm, but it's all Portuguese to *me*! . . . And wagged his Persian tail."

" Go on."

" One evening," she went on, " while Madame Orio was fast asleep in her little belvedere (it being the good old lady's habit to repair there to rest after a bottle or two of red Padua wine), Manette and Marton left the widow's house noiselessly in the Campo San Zobenigo, and made their way running towards the Piazza of St. Mark's. It was a radiant night in early April. All Venice was in the open air. The moon, which——"

Listening with detached attention lest her ears should be seduced and tickled rather than soundly chastened, Mrs. Hurstpierpoint's mind turned somewhat sombrely to her future connection with her heir's fiancée. Some opinionated, wrong-headed creature, *une femme mal pensante*, in the house, she mused, would be indeed tormenting. While on the other hand, of course, Dick's bride *might* add a new interest to the place; in which case Elizabeth's attitude too would be sure to change.

Mrs. Hurstpierpoint plied speculatively her beads, catching between her *Aves* just enough of the tale to be able to follow its drift.

Music, she heard. Those sisters ✠ a ripe and rich marquesa ✠ strong proclivities ✠ a white starry plant ✠ water ✠ lanterns ✠ little streets ✠ Il Redentore ✠ Pasqualino ✠ behind the Church of ✠ Giudecca ✠ gondola ✠ Lido ✠ Love ✠ lagoon ✠ Santa Orsola ✠ the Adriatic——

With a sigh at the mutability of things, she realised that with a young daughter-in-law of her own Elizabeth would no longer be towards her her same gracious self. With the advent of Dick's wife a potential disturbing force would enter Hare. New joy would bring new sorrow. Whoever he might choose to marry, intrigue, jealousy would seldom be far away. Should Gilda Vintage be the *partie*, then Lady Parvula de

Panzoust with her irrelevant souvenirs would be a constant figure at Hare: she would "come over" probably quite easily—sooner, even, than her daughter! "And her *First* Confession," Mrs. Hurstpierpoint ruminated with a crucial, fleeting smile, "if (by some little harmless strategy) I could arrange it, I should dearly love to hear!"

Her cogitations were interrupted by the return of Mrs. Thoroughfare, leading by the hand a reluctant Poor Clare for a cup of tea.

Proscribed by her Order to Silence, and having nothing in her physiognomy to help her out, Sister Ecclesia's position at present was one of peculiar difficulty and constraint.

In the Convent of Arimathæa, at Sodbury hard by Hare whence she came, her indiscreet talkativeness had impelled a wise, if severe, Mother-Superior to impose upon her the *Torture* of Silence—which supplice had led her inevitably into tricks; Sister Ecclesia had contracted mannerisms therefrom. Though uttering no audible word her lips seldom were still. Strangers sometimes took her to be a saint, in touch with heaven. Bursting to speak she would frequently, when in society, shake clenched hands in the air impotently like a child. Sometimes, in order to find an outlet to her pent emotions, she would go as far as to kick and to pinch, and even to dance (her spirited hornpipes with Captain Thoroughfare were much admired at Hare), while with a broomstick she was invaluable—a very tigress—drawing blood directly. Indeed, as Mrs. Hurstpierpoint was wont to say, her arm seemed born for a birch. Thrice a year Sister Ecclesia was allowed the use of her tongue when instead of seeking intercourse among the nuns she would flit off quite alone towards the sea-shore and blend her voice with the errant gulls until her unrestrained cries and screams frequently caused her to faint.

With vacuous, half-closed lids, Mrs. Hurstpierpoint accepted her generous shower-bath of Eau Benite.

"Out? Already," she murmured, simultaneously offering her hand on one side while abandoning her lips on the other.

"And oh! Eulalia," Mrs. Thoroughfare's voice shook with inflections, "who should one find in Nuestra Señora . . . (in the Capella Love of the Salutation) but Lady Violet Logg? Lady Violet! Elegant to tears, and with two such wisps of boys! Boys of about seventeen—or eighteen, Eulalia! Like the mignons of Henry the Third."

"I suppose . . . no umbrella."

"And I am sure that Edie's pricked."

"I know of more than one in the house to be wobbling!" Fowler averred as with rush-like gait at the view of the butler's crane-like legs, harbinger of the tea-board (in the dark of his mind might he not aspire to build with her? Swoop! Fly to church with her: make a nest of her? Snatch at her? Bend her, break her—God knew how!—to his passions' uses?), she flexibly withdrew.

"If anyone calls, ffines," Mrs. Hurstpierpoint said, rousing herself and running a hand to her half-falling hair, "better simply say I'm out."

"Les-bia—ah-h . . .!" Mrs. Thoroughfare struck a few chords airily on the open piano.

"And, ffines . . . an extra cup."

"An extra, 'm?"

"Insensate!"

"Hitherto 'm (and I've seen some choice service I am sure) I always gave entire satisfaction."

"You never saw choicer service (I am quite sure) than with *me*, ffines," Mrs. Hurstpierpoint said, complacently adjusting a pin. "And I'd have you to remember it!"

"Julia, Duchess of Jutland thought the world of me."

"And so do I, ffines. I think the world of you too —*this* world! . . ."

"White Mit-y-lene . . ." Mrs. Thoroughfare broke melodiously in, "where the gir——"

"What was that song about lilacs, Lizzie?" Mrs. Hurstpierpoint, turning to her, asked.

"*Lilacs*, Eulalia?"

"Something to do with lilacs: *lilacs en fleur;* an old air of France."

"Le temps des lilas et le temps des roses,
Ne reviendra plus à ce printemps ci.
Le temps de lilas et les temps des roses
Est passé, le temps des œillets aussi.

Le vent a changé les cieux sont moroses,
Et nous n'irons plus courir et cueillir
Les lilas en fleur et les belles roses;
Le printemps est triste et ne peut fleurir.

Oh, joyeux et doux printemps de l'année
Qui vint, l'an passé, nous ensoleiller,
Notre fleur d'amour est si bien fanée.
Las! que ton baiser ne peut l'eveiller.

Et toi, que fais-tu? pas de fleurs écloses,
Point de gai soleil ni d'ombrages frais;
Le temps des lilas et le temps des roses
Avec notre amour est mort à jamais."

Mrs. Thoroughfare's voice ebbed.

"May a woman know, dear," Mrs. Hurstpierpoint softly said, "when she may receive her drubbing?"

"Oh I've no strength left in me to-day, Eulalia, I fear, for anything," Mrs. Thoroughfare answered.

" Positively? "

" Ask Ecclesia! "

But with the French song over Sister Ecclesia had edged, with much wild grace, from the room.

" She's returned to her prayers, I suppose."

" Or to Father."

" Happily, quite in vain! "

" *Chè volete?* "

" I miss Père Ernest," Mrs. Hurstpierpoint sighed, leisurely sipping her tea.

" Yes, dear, but he had too many ultramontane habits. . . . There was really no joy in pouring out one's sins while he sat assiduously picking his nose."

" Which reminds me," Mrs. Hurstpierpoint serenely said, " to gather my nectarines. . . ."

" Your nectarines . . .? "

" Sir Victor begs me for a few nectarine models. Nectarines meet to sit to him. Not *too* ripe."

" I should think he only wanted them for himself," Mrs. Thoroughfare cooed, opening wide a window that commanded an outlook of the lawns.

The atmosphere was clearer now. Before the house the mutilated statues and widowed urns showed palely white against a sky palely blue through which a rainbow was fast forming. By the little garden pergola open to the winds some fluttered peacocks were blotted nervelessly amid the dripping trees, their heads sunk back beneath their wings: while in the pergola itself, like a fallen storm-cloud, lolled a negress, her levelled, polecat eyes semi-veiled by the nebulous alchemy of the rainbow.

" What are you doing fiddle-faddling over there, Elizabeth? " Mrs. Hurstpierpoint asked.

" Look, Eulalia," Mrs. Thoroughfare said, catching her breath; "some one with a kite is on our lawn!"

Mrs. Hurstpierpoint was impelled to smile.

" In the old days," she murmured, brushing a few

65

crumbs from her gown, " sailing a kite heavenward was my utmost felicity. No ball of string, I remember, was ever long enough! "

" This is no christian and her kite, Eulalia, or I'm much mistaken. . . ."

" No christian, Elizabeth? "

" It's a savage."

Mrs. Hurstpierpoint sank humbly to her knees.

" *Gloria in Excelsis tibi Deo!* " she solemnly exclaimed.

VII

THE plaintive pizzicato of Madame Mimosa's Pom pup "Plum-Bun" aroused Mrs. Yajñavalkya one triumphal summer morning while lying in the voluminous feather-bed that since lately she shared with her niece.

"*Zbaffa pbf!*" she complained, addressing an ape-like image, cut in jade, that stood at the bed-end, its incensed arms and elongated eyes defensively alert. Beside her Niri-Esther, indiscreetly *enceinte*, was still asleep.

"O de worries!" the negress murmured, leaving indolently her bed and hitching higher the blind.

It was a Market morning. . . . Beneath a mottled sky some score or so of little carts covered in frail tarpaulins of unnamable sun-scorched colours were mustered before the Daleman Memorial where already a certain amount of petty chicanery had begun.

"Dat is a scene now which somehow make me smile," Mrs. Yajñavalkya commented. "Ya Allah, but whenever I see a Market I no longer feel Abroad. . . . And w'y, I wonder, is de reason ob dis? . . Because human nature is de same ebberywhere."

"Any old flint glass or broken bottles for a poor woman to-day?" a barrow-hawker smote into her reflections from below.

Mrs. Yajñavalkya indrew her head.

It was one of her fullest mornings, being the eve of Mrs. Hurstpierpoint's reunion in honour of the centenarians of the place, who together with their progeny assembled yearly in the closed drawing-rooms, or beneath the titanic cedars, of Hare.

Andfor these annual resuscitations Mrs. Yajñavalkya's invigorating touch was deemed almost indispensable.

Consulting her tablets, she found Tooke's Farm to be first on her list, when it might be that the dairyman himself would be about. Disheartening contretemps had followed hitherto her every intriguing effort. He had responded to her summons to " take a look at the Vine " in the small grape-house at the extremity of the garden, politely, if unorthodoxly enough, bringing with him, with Mrs. Tooke's " compliments," a sumptuous barrowful of well-seasoned offal, whereat Lady Parvula de Panzoust, poised like a Bacchante amid the drooping grapes, had taken to fastidious heels in alarm.

" If I cannot throw dem both together," she brooded, " be it only out ob doors . . . I will be obliged to quench lub's fever wif a sedative."

The venerable dial of St. Veronica's wood clock, and a glimpse of Nurse Yates' under-sized form crossing the Square, advised her not to dawdle, and soon she, too, was threading her way amid the arguing yokels and the little carts.

Beneath a strip of awning that shook slightly in the soft sea air a sailor with eyes like sad sapphires was showing a whale caught in the bay, to view which he asked a penny. Partially hid within a fishing creel it brought back to Mrs. Yajñavalkya the unfaithful wives of her own native land who were cast as a rule to the sharks.

Refusing payment only to revive poignant memories of aunts and cousins, sisters and sisters-in-law, as well as a close escape of her own, Mrs. Yajñavalkya disdainfully moved away.

In a cottage garden at the corner of the market-place she could distinguish the sexton of St. Veronica's meandering round his beehives in a white paper mask. From his shuffling step and obvious air of preoccupa-

68

tion, it was as though in some instinctive way he was aware that the consequences of the Hare-Hatch rout would shortly drive him to " resume " his spade.

Flitting fleetly by, Mrs. Yajñavalkya attained the weather-beaten farmyard gate where, grinning as he watched her approach, stood Bobby Jolly.

" Is your master in, you little giggling Valmouth goose? " she inquired.

" David? He won't be back till evenfall."

" Oho? "

" He's felling trees in Wingley Woo," the child replied, looking up quizzically into the negress's face.

Between his long curly lashes were blue eyes—not very deep: a slight down, nearly white, sprouted below a dainty little nose, just above the lip at the two corners.

" No matter. So long as the dear dowager has not gone with him," Mrs. Yajñavalkya replied, jauntily entering the yard. On the dung-hill that rose against the church to the sill of the clerestory-windows lay Douce—treacherously asleep, his muzzle couched on a loose forepaw.

" He leave behind him de dog? "

" 'Cos of pheasants."

Mrs. Yajñavalkya shaded her brow from the sun with her hand.

Through an open barn she could trace the River Val winding leisurely coastward through cornfields white with glory. A hum of bees from the flower plat by the garden wall filled the air with a ceaseless sound and raised the mind up to Allah.

She chanced on Mrs. Tooke essaying the effect of a youthful little cap before the glass.

" Charming," the negress cried. " Delicious! "

Decked with silk bandstrings and laces, the old lady's long bluish profile, calcined on the grave-ground without, recalled to Mrs. Yajñavalkya one

of the incomparable Dutch paintings assigned to
Franz Hals, in Evadne, Duchess of Valmouth's
boudoir.

" Faith, my dear," Mrs. Tooke exclaimed, " but you
frightened me."

" And how do you find yourself, Mrs. Tooke, to-
day? " the negress archly asked.

Troubled at being surprised in an act of vanity, a
thing she professed to abhor, Mrs. Tooke was inclined
to be captious.

" To-day I feel only passably well, Mrs. Yaj," she
replied.

" I've seen you worse, Mrs. Tooke."

" I fear I shall soon become now a portion for foxes."

" Dat is for me to say, Mrs. Tooke."

" I ha'n't the constitution at all that I had."

" De prospect ob a function may have occasioned
a touch ob fever; nothing but a little cerebral excite-
ment, de outcome ob neurasthenia, which my methods,
I hope, will remove."

" I wish I hadn't a wen, Mrs. Yaj! A sad hash your
methods made of it."

" De more you cauterise a wen, Mrs. Tooke . . .
Besides, wot's de good ob worry? Not poppy, nor
mandragora, nor all the drowsy syrups of the world,
shall ever soothe it or medicine it away. Remember."

Mrs. Tooke sighed submissively.

"Where did I put my Bible? " she plaintively asked,
peering around the long-familiar room.

" I wonder you're not tired ob your Bible, Mrs.
Tooke."

" Fie! Mrs. Yaj. You shouldn't speak so."

" You should read de Talmud for a change "

" It sounds a poor exchange."

" Do you really believe now, Mrs. Tooke my dear,
in de Apostolic Succession? Can you look me in de
eyes and say you do? "

70

" I ha'n't paid any heed lately to those chaps, Mrs. Yaj; I'm going on to Habakkuk."

" Was not he de companion ob de Prodigal son? "

" Maybe he was, my dear. He seems to have known a good many people."

" Dat is not de name now ob a man, Mrs. Tooke, to observe a single wife, nor even a single sex. . . . No! Oh no; a man wif a name like dat would have his needs! "

" Heysey-ho! We most of us have our wants."

" From all one hears, Mrs. Tooke, your grandson hasn't many."

" Yoiks Mrs. Yaj! He was at me just now for a Bull."

" And do you tell me so, Mrs. Tooke? "

" A farm's no farm without a Bull, says he; and t'other day 'twas a shorthorn milcher he'd have had me buy."

" He seems insensitive to women, Mrs. Tooke! I think, my dear, he never was truly enmeshed."

" He's unimpressionable, I'm thankful to say."

" I know ob one now, Mrs. Tooke, who would be glad to be on his two legs again to-morrow night— and who *will* be, my dear, I dare say, although I did refuse him."

Mrs. Tooke evinced detachment.

" They tell me Doris Country's dress is being edged with ermine," she observed, fastening her eye on a piece of old Valmouth ware representing a dog with a hen in its mouth, that occupied the dresser.

" You'll need your *boa* as de nights are chilly."

" 'Od: I've no ermine skin myself! "

" Dair are furs besides ermine, Mrs. Tooke. Wot is dair smarter dan a monkey's tail trimmed in black lace?—wid no stint mind to de strings; dat is a combination dat always succeed."

" Belike."

71

" In my land ermine, you know, is exclusive to de khan or, as you would say, de king."

" His Majesty, the Can! " the old lady shyly marvelled.

" He my beloved sovereign."

" And your Queens (I presume) are Pitchers? "

" Never you mind now, Mrs. Tooke, never you mind! but just let me rub a little ob dis on de seat ob your ovaries; de same as I did once to a Muscovite princess. . . . ' Your magic hand, my dear,' she say, ' it bring such joy and release. . . .' "

" I wish I had your brawn, Mrs. Yaj! "

" Noble, or ignoble, Mrs. Tooke, I treat my clients just de same! "

" You old black bogey, what should I do without you? "

" *Inshallah!* " The negress shrugged, glancing over her shoulder at a sudden sneeze from Miss Tooke behind her.

Bearing in her arms the sacrificial linen, she waded forward in a ray of dusty sunlight, as if fording in fancy the turbid Val that should transport her to Love's transcendent delights, in illimitable, jewelly seas.

" It's a hard thing, Mrs. Yaj," Mrs. Tooke observed, " to be dependent on a wench who spends half her life in the river! If *I* was a fish I'd snap at her legs."

" I've no doubt you would, Mrs. Tooke, but joking, my dear, apart, unless as a finish to a douche cold water I always discommend. Dair (in moderation no doubt) it is good; otherwise in my opinion it is injurious to de circulation, impeding and clogging de natural channels and so hampering de course ob de blood, and often even gibbing excuse to de body's worst enemy ob all—I mean de gastric juices."

Mrs. Tooke's brows knit together. She scowled.

" Let her keep her distance," she exclaimed, " with her contagious heavy cold! "

" I am sure I've no will to come near you," Miss Tooke replied with a desolating sigh as she fell to earth.

She was looking restless and pale and strangely avid for love.

" You'll not die in an old skin if you fret it so, Thetis girl, ah, that ye won't."

" What's the use of living then? Life is only acceptable on the condition that it is enjoyed."

Mrs. Tooke blinked, eluded.

" Belike," she said, " by God's grace to-morrow night we'll both have a bit of a fling. Oh-ay, I do mind the nestful of field-mice we had in the spring-cart last year. I had been out all day among the clover, but, Lord! I never knew 'twas full of they mice, till a satire, in livery, shoved his hand (like a sauce-box) into the cart, under pretext of helping me down, when pouf! out they all hopped from under my train, furnishing the tag-rag and bobtail there was standing about with all manner of *immund* remarks. . . ."

" And where was this, Mrs. Tooke? " the negress aloofly asked.

" Why at Hare, Mrs. Yaj, last year."

Miss Tooke sighed again, and drawing a cut citron from her apron pocket she applied it gently (as directed by " Susuva " in *The Woman's Friend*) to the roots of her nails.

> " When I am dead
> Ah bring me flow-ers,
> Spread roses and forget-me-nots,"

she somewhat hectically hummed.

" You bits of raw shoots seldom hark to any sense, though 'twere better often to be a primrose in the wilderness than a polyanthus in a frame. And you'll remember, maybe, I said so, when I'm grassed down

73

in the earth and gone," Mrs. Tooke declared, riveting her attention on the tombstones below.

Several of the nearer epitaphs were distinctly legible through the farmstead windows, such as "*Josephine —first wife of Q. Comedy Esqre died of Jealousy, March 31st 1898: Remember her*," while the rest, monotonously identical, for the most part betokened " inconsolable widows " and were nothing, according to Mrs. Tooke (who had eyes for a wedding as well as for a funeral), but "a ' —— ' tangle of lies! " One gaunt, tall cross, however, half hidden by conifers, a little apart, almost isolated, solitary, alone, was, to the excellent Englishwoman, in its provocativeness, as a chalk egg is to a sensitive hen. Here lay Balty Vincent Wise, having lived and died—*unmarried*. Oh what a funny fellow! Oh what a curious man! . . . What did he mean by going off like that? Was no woman good enough for him then? Oh what a queer reflection to be sure; what a slur on all her sex! Oh but he should have settled; ranged himself as every bachelor should! Improper naughty thing! He should be exorcised and whipped: or had he loved? Loved perchance *elsewhere* . . .? The subject of many a fluttered reverie he gave, by his eccentric manes, just that touch of mystery, that piquant interest to the churchyard that inwardly she loved—Balty!

" There are times, Mrs. Yaj, when I find the lookout cheerless."

" Still! Radder dan see ' Marsh-lights ' . . ."

" Ah . . . I shall never forget how Mr. Comedy (when he lost his first wife) passed the night in the graveyard, crying and singing and howling, with a magnum of Mumm. . . ."

With a wry little laugh Miss Tooke turned and moved away.

" Since you've all, then, you need," she said, " I'll take a pail of clams and yams, I think, to feed the pigs."

74

" Let 'em farrow if they choose, and keep clear of the river, mind; don't let me hear of you in the Val again to-day."

" The Val! You ought to see the Ganges, Mrs. Tooke! Ah, dat is some river indeed."

" In what way, Mrs. Yaj? "

" A girl may loiter there with her amphora and show her ankles to de fleets of sailing sampans often to her advantage. . . . Many a match-making mother have I known, my dear, to send her daughter to stand below some eligible Villa with instructions to toy for an hour with her crock."

" As I'm a decent widow, Mrs. Yaj, you negresses are a bad lot, I'm afraid."

" O w'y? "

" I expect it's something to do with your climate."

" We Eastern women love the sun . . . ! When de thermometer rise to some two hundred or so, ah dat is de time to lie among de bees and canes."

" I could never stand the stew——, it would take all *my* stamina."

" My little maid, Carry, is de same as you. De least spell ob warmth prostrate her wid de vertigoes."

" You've had her some time now, Mrs. Yaj."

" So I have, Mrs. Tooke, so I have; dô I say often I've a mind to take a page; but a growing boy in de house, my dear—you *know* what dey are! However, Carry I soon shall have to dismiss. . . . She dat otiose! She dat idle! She will read by de hour from my medical dictionary, dô I defend her eber to open it, because dair are tings she is perhaps better without de knowledge ob! *Kra.* And how she wreck my china! Before I came to dis place I had no stylish services; but I would go out and pick myself a plate ob a fresh green leaf, and den wen it had served its purpose, after each course, I would just throw it away; and like dat dair was no expense, and none ob dese breakages at all."

75

"Well, there are plenty of pleasant trees round Valmouth, Mrs. Yaj, I'm sure; and you're welcome to flower-leaf or vegetable from these acres, my dear, at any time; you shall sup off Dock a-Monday, and Cabbage Tuesday, Violet-hearts on Wednesday, Ivy Thursday, Nettle Friday, King Solomon's seal Saturday, and Sunday, you old black caterpillar, you can range as you please through the grass."

"I have my own little garden, Mrs. Tooke, my dear, you forget: but dat white calf now out yonder . . . my niece beg me to say she'd buy it, as she desire to sacrifice it to a certain goddess for private family reasons."

"For shame, Mrs. Yaj. It makes me sad to hear you talk like a heathen."

"Such narrow prejudice; for I suppose it will only go to de butcher in de end?"

"Disgusting."

"Butchers are so brutal, Mrs. Tooke . . . ! Dair hearts must be so unkind . . . men without mercy! And dat's wot I alvays say."

"Ts!"

"And remember dis, my dear. It is for her deity and not for herself she seek the calf."

"Be quiet."

"Niri-Esther only relish roots, a dish ob white roots and fruits—unless dis last few day, when she express a fancy for water-melon jam! But where I say in Valmouth can you find water-melon jam? O de worries, Mrs. Tooke!"

"I ha'n't seen her kite so much lately, Mrs. Yaj."

"Babies are so tender. . . . Little children are so frail . . ." the negress said to herself aloud.

"What's that, my dear?"

"I miss a mosque, Mrs. Tooke, and de consolation ob de church; but when I turn to Allah, I suppose de Holy Mihrab near to me and den," the negress mur-

mured, bestowing a parting pinch upon the aged dame,
" all is well."

Her day indeed was but begun. In many a cloud-
swept village bespattering the hills her presence was
due anon.

Issuing from the farm-house she hovered to consider the itinerary ahead—culminating picturesquely
(towards sunset) in a ruined stomach—some six miles
from the town. Deliberatingly traversing the yard,
where, here and there, fowl were pecking negligently
at their shadows, she recognised in the penumbra of a
cart-shed the arrowy form of Lady Parvula de Panzoust.

She wore a dress of becoming corduroy and a hat
all rose-pink feathers, the little basket upon her arm
signifying, evidently—*eggs*.

Following her (with more perhaps than his habitual
suspicion) was churlish Douce.

" Poor, dear, beautiful, patient beast! " the negress
could hear her say in tones of vivacious interest as
she fondled the dog's supple back and long, soft,
nervelessly drooping ears. Then suddenly stooping,
she exclaimed vehemently, as if transported: " Kiss
me, Bushy! "

VIII

It was the auspicious night when as to a Sabbat the centenarians of Valmouth, escorted by twittering troops of expectant heirs and toad-eating relatives, foregathered together, like so many warlocks and witches, in the generously loaned drawing-rooms and corridors of Hare.

Originating in the past with the corporation, as a subtle advertisement to the salubrity of the climate, these reunions were now in such high favour that the Valmouth Town Hall, a poor poky place, was no longer capable of holding so numerous an attendance, obliging the municipality to seek a more convenient rendezvous elsewhere; hence the cordial offer of the Hare ladies to " throw open " their doors annually had been accepted officially with a thousand pleasant thanks; and by degrees, by dint of some acted *Mystery*, played to perfection by the Nuns of Sodbury and the Oblates of Up-More, these reunions had afforded full scope for the diplomatic furtherance of Rome.

Something of Limbo, perhaps, was felt by those at present gathered in the long salon, bafflingly lit by an old-fashioned chain-chandelier that threw all the light upwards, towards the ceiling, leaving the room below (to the untold relief of some) in semi-obscurity; but, the night being fine, many preferred to wander out attracted by the silken streamers of a vast marquee.

Leaning on the arm of a swathed tangerine figure, Mrs. Hurstpierpoint, decked in wonderful pearls like Titian's Queen of Cyprus, trailed about beneath the mounting moon, greeting here and there a contemporary with vague cognition. She seemed in charming spirits.

78

"Your ladyship dribbles!" she complacently commented, shaking from the curling folds of her dress a pious leaflet, *The —— of Mary*, audaciously scouting the Augustinian theory "that the Blessed Virgin conceived our Lord through the Ears."

Looking demurely up she saw wide azure spaces stabbed with stars like many Indian pinks.

The chimeric beauty of the night was exhilarating.

In the heavy blooming air the rolling, moon-lit lawns and great old toppling trees stretched away, interfusing far off into soft deeps of velvet, dark blue violet, void.

"The last time I went to the play," the tangerine figure fluted, "was with Charles the Second and Louise de Querouaille, to see Betterton play Shylock in *The Merchant of Venice*."

"Was he so fine?" Mrs. Hurstpierpoint asked, her query drowned in a dramatic dissonance from the pergola—climax to a blood-stirring waltz.

On the lawn-sward couples were revolving beneath the festooned trees that twinkled convivially with fairy-lamps, but the centre of attraction, perhaps, at present was the Mayor.

"Congratulations," his voice pealed out, "to Peggy Laugher, Ann and Zillah Bottom, Almeria Goatpath, Thisbe Brownjohn, Teresa Twistleton, Rebecca Bramblebrook, Junie Jones, Susannah Sneep, Peter Palafox, Flo Flook, Simon Toole, Molly Ark, Nellie Knight, Fanny Beard, May Thatcher, May Heaven, George Kissington, Tircis Tree, Gerry Bosboom, Gilbert Soham, Lily Quickstep, Doris Country, Anna Clootz, Mary Teeworthy, Dorothy Tooke, Patrick Flynn, Rosa Sweet, Laurette Venum, Violet Ebbing, Horace Hardly, Mary Wilks——."

"*In saeculum saeculi*, apparently!" Mrs. Hurstpierpoint shrugged.

On the fringe of the throng, by a marble shape of

Priapus green with moss, Lady Parvula de Panzoust was listening, as if petrified at her thoughts, to the Mayor.

"I shall never forget her," the tangerine bundle breathed, "one evening at Salsomaggiore——!"

"For a fogy, she's not half bad, is she, still?"

"I consider her a charming, persuasive, still beautiful, and *always* licentious woman. . . ."

"And with the art . . . not of returning thistles for figs?"

"There are rumours—I dare say you know—of an affair here in the town."

"Poor Parvula . . .! a scandal, more or less, it will make no difference to her whatever," Mrs. Hurstpierpoint answered lucidly, turning apprehensively at the sound of a jocose laugh from Mrs. Yajñavalkya.

Très affairée, equipped in silk of Broussa, she was figurable perhaps to nothing so much as something from below.

"That little black niece of hers, my dear, is extremely exciting. . . ."

"Divinely voluptuous."

Mrs. Hurstpierpoint tossed a troubled leaflet.

"She is ravishing," she declared, wafting a butterfly kiss to the Abbess of Sodbury—Mère Marie de Cœurbrisé. Née a Begby of "Bloxworth," Mère Marie's taste for society was innate, and her petits goûters in the convent parlour were amazing institutions, if Sister Ecclesia, before her lips were bound, was to be believed.

"It puts me in mind of Vauxhall when I was a girl," she chuckled.

"Oh—oh!"

"*Wunderschön! Bella, bella.*"

Her old orchidised face, less spiritualised than orchidised by the convent walls, in the moonlight seemed quite blue.

" And my birch, the blessed broom. . . . Is it in
Italy? Has His Holiness complied with the almond-
twigs? " Mrs. Hurstpierpoint inquired, drawing her
away just as Mrs. Yajñavalkya, believing the leaflet to
be as fraught with meaning as a Sultan's handkerchief,
dispatched her niece to pick it up.

Such an unorthodox mode of introduction could
not but cause the heart a tremor.

" In de case ob future advance," Mrs. Yajñavalkya
enjoined her niece (smiling impenetrably at her
thoughts), " be sure to say de dear billet shall receive
your prompt attention."

" Paia! " Niri-Esther assented.

She was looking vanquishing in a transparent,
sleeveless tunic, over a pair of rose-mauve knickers of
an extraordinary intensity of hue. In her arms she held
a sheaf of long-stemmed, pearl-white roses—*Soif de
Tendresse.*

" We shall enter de palace by de garden gate . . .
by de gate ob de garden . . ." Mrs. Yajñavalkya
reflected, her eyes embracing the long, semi-Grecian
outline of the house.

Before the mask-capped windows, Lady Parvula de
Panzoust pointed sharply the dusk with a shimmering fan.

" Your Diana," the negress, approaching, coughed,
" we speak ob as Hina. But she is de same; she is de
moon."

" Ah? "

" She is de moon. . . ."

" Soon, again, she'll be dwindling."

" May you enjoy ambrosia: a lover's tigerish kisses,
ere she disappears."

Lady Parvula braced nervously her shoulders.

" Who is the woman in the cerements? " she in-
consequently wondered.

" Dat dair she some stranger."

" It amuses one to watch their dying flutters. . . ."

"You should take notice ob de wife ob de Mayor. Dô she be a hundred and forty, and more, yet she hardly look de age ob ' consent '! "

"Have you nothing else—more interesting—to tell me? " Lady Parvula asked, motioning to the shade of the nearest tree.

"Assuredly," the negress answered, following towards the dark-spreading Spina-Christi over against the house.

I, I, I, I! A night-bird fled on startled wings.

"Like the cry of an injured man! " Lady Parvula murmured, sinking composedly to a garden chair.

"Like de cry ob a djinn! "

"Well; is one any nearer? does he seem in a coming-on stage? " her ladyship blithely asked.

The oriental woman swelled.

"De way he questioned me concerning you, milady," she unctuously made reply, " was enough to make a swan bury its head beneath de water."

"Silly fellow and is he crazy about me, you say? Dear boy. Well."

"He say he ready to eat you."

"To—what? "

"Ah de rogue! "

"Eat me . . . and when does he wish to devour me? " Lady Parvula touched nervously the white plumes and emeralds in the edifice of her hair.

"Ah de wretch! "

"Doesn't he say? "

"Al-ways he is hungry, de ogre! "

"The great, big, endless fellow! "

"Al-ways he is clamouring for a meal."

"Let him guard as he can those ambered freckles! "

"Dey would draw de mazy bees."

"I so feared he was going to be shy." With pensive psychic fingers the enamoured Englishwoman toyed with a talismanic bagatelle in New Zealand jade.

82

" Believe me, he only play de part ob de timid youth de better to surprise you."

" Simple angel! "

" He resist."

" I once made a grand resistance—and oh! don't I regret it now . . . the poor dear was of low birth: humble origin: no condition: my husband's amanu- ensis! But oh! oh ! ! "

" Dose villain valets. Dey are de very men wif dair fair hard hair and dair chiselled faces. . . ."

" This was a paid secretary. . . . But oh, oh! Even my Lord. He could hardly spell. . . ."

" His face was his fortune? "

" Possibly. But I never was careless of appearances, as I told you I think once before. To my good name I cling. Mine, I congratulate myself, is entirely proof. No one has ever really been able to make a heroine out of me! The bordomette of circumlocution one submits to meekly perforce. In the Happy East you live untrammelled by the ghouls of our insular con- vention."

Mrs. Yajñavalkya shook a stiff forefinger.

" Sho," she muttered, allowing soft, discarnate voices to articulate and move on.

" Her great regret you know . . ." the murmur came, "she is . . . God forgive her . . . the former Favour- ite of a king; although, as she herself declares, *only* for a few minutes. Poor darling! . . . Yes! My poor Love! She gave herself to an *earthly* crown. . . ."

" An ex-mistress of a king: she has the air."

" It is Eulalia's *constant torment!* " The voices ebbed.

Lady Parvula looked down at the blue winter- violets in the front of her dress.

" Her sway was short! " she wondered.

She was all herself in a gown of pale brocade with a banana pattern in gold fibre breaking all over it.

" In an affair ob kismet—for it is kismet; what (I

83

ask you to tell me) is reputation? What is it, reputation, in a case ob dis discription? Dis Smara. Dis Mektoub. Dis Destiny! "

" Sound him again. Put out final feelers," Lady Parvula murmured, waving dismissal with a tap of her fan.

With a wise expressive nod the negress turned away.

Picking her way over the contorted roots of the trees she shaped her course towards the house, pausing to admire a universe of stars in a marble basin drip drop dripping, drip drip dropping, over with the clearest water.

" Væa, væa," she mused, " satufa lu-lu fiss."

Looking up she perceived David Tooke, as if in ambush behind a statue of Meleager that resembled himself.

" Vot do you dair so unsocial? " she demanded in her softest gavroche speaking voice.

The young yeoman smiled slowly.

" Is it true," he abstrusely answered, " that in your country bulls consort with mares, and rams seek after cows, and the males of partridges do curious things among themselves."

" Whoebber told you so told lies."

" Told lies? "

" Dey told you only ob de few exceptions."

" Ah."

He seemed a trifle moonstruck.

" But ob vot importance is it? . . . Suppose *dey do*? Come on now, and hitch your wagon to a star."

" I'll hitch my wagon where I choose."

" Up wid dose dear shafts."

" Tiddy-diddy-doll! " ungraciously he hummed.

" You marry her—and be a Lord! "

" Be off! Don't pester me."

" Come on now."

" Heart and belly: not I! "

" Must I *pull* you? "

" Pull me? "

" Drag you to milady."

" Don't make me a scene, because my nerves can't stand it! "

" Vas dair ebber a eunuch like you? "

" Why does she want to come bothering me? "

" I have nebber heard of such contempt ob de peerage," Mrs. Yajñavalkya fairly snorted.

" Here's Granny," he breathed.

And indeed rounding a garden path on her grand-daughter's arm Mrs. Tooke was making a spirited progress of the grounds.

" Glad am I, my dear," the negress cried, " to see you're still so able . . ."

" Isht! My legs gae all tapsalteerie! "

" Dat is nothing but Nature's causes. What is wobblyness ever but de outcome simply ob disuse? "

" Just hark to my joints! I'm positively tumbling to bits! "

" And where are you off to, Mrs. Tooke? "

" To make a beau-pot, Mrs. Yaj."

" What do you call a *beau-pot*, Mrs. Tooke? "

" A posy, Mrs. Yaj."

" And vot's a posy, Mrs. Tooke? "

" A bunch of flowers, my dear."

" In de East dair is a rose, deep and red, dat wen she open go off, pop, pop, pop—like de crack ob a gun! " and relinquishing her quarry, with a meaning glance, the negress strolled away.

" He is frigid. Dat I will admit: and bearish a little, too. But de boy is not such a fool," she philosophised, gazing around her for a sign of her niece.

Through a yew-hedge, thinner at the bottom than at the top, she could see the feet of the dancers as they came and went.

85

A drowsy Tzigane air, intricate, caressing, vibrated sensuously to the night.

" May I have the pleasure . . .? " a mild-faced youth, one of the Oblates of Up-More, addressed her.

" Delighted," she answered, with equanimity, accepting his arm.

" Your countrywoman doesn't dance," he observed, signalising Niri-Esther astride the seat-board of a garden swing, attached to the aerial branches of a silver fir.

She was clinging mysteriously to the ropes as though her instinct told her they had known the pressure of the palms of someone not altogether indifferent to her heart.

" Just at present . . ." the negress shrugged, submitting to be borne off by the will of a man.

"Ga—ga," Niri-Esther gurgled, rubbing her cheek languorously against the cord.

" A push is it? " Mrs. Hurstpierpoint aborded her with a smile. " Is it a push you wish for, dear child? Is that," she dismantlingly ogled, " what you're after?" and taking silence for assent, she resolutely clasped the black girl from behind below the middle.

Niri-Esther fetched a shout.

" Oh! Eulalia! ! ! " Mrs. Thoroughfare approached à pas de loup. " What are you up to, Eulalia? What are you doing? "

" Go away, Thoroughfare. Now, go away."

" Oh, Eulalia." Mrs. Thoroughfare shrank.

" Is not that heavenly, dear child? " the formidable woman queried, depositing a rich muff of Carrickmacross lace, bulging with propaganda, upon the ground.

" Stop! "

" Was not that divine, my dear? Didn't you like it? " The hieratic woman pressed, passing her tongue with quiet but evident relish along her upper lip.

86

Niri-Esther turned aside her head.

The constipated whiteness of a peacock in the penumbra of the tree was disquieting to her somewhat.

" Bird!! " Mrs. Hurstpierpoint chuckled.

" Ours at home are much bigger."

" Are they, dear child? "

" Much."

" I want us to be friends. Will you? "

" Why? "

" Ah, my dear . . . ' why '? Because," Mrs. Hurstpierpoint quavered, leaning forward to inhale the singularly pungent perfume proceeding from the negress's person, " because you're very lovable."

" Eulalia! " Mrs. Thoroughfare reimportunated.

" Yes, Elizabeth! "

" I'm anxious to speak to you for a moment privately, Eulalia."

" Well——"

" Oh, Eulalia! " Mrs. Thoroughfare faltered. "Madame Mimosa is here . . . exercising her calling . . ."

" What? "

" Oh, Eulalia. . . ."

" ffines! And turn her out."

" At least, darling, she was arm-in-arm . . . entwined, Eulalia."

" Prude Elizabeth. Was that all you had to say? "

Mrs. Thoroughfare cast a grim glance towards Niri-Esther.

" Oh, she's a monstrous kid, Eulalia! . . . Isn't she just ? "

" I don't agree with you there, Elizabeth, at all."

" Oh, she's a nutty girl; she's a bit of all right."

" Why are you so down on her, Eliza? "

" I, Eulalia? I'm not down. I think her charming."

" I'm glad you do."

" She has her immaturity. I divine this and that."

" Pho."

" I guess a great deal."

" How dear Richard would have admired her."

" Dick would? How? "

Mrs. Hurstpierpoint lifted her shoulders slightly.

" Your son has a many-sided nature to him, Elizabeth," she observed; " which I suppose is not sur-
prising when one thinks of you! "

" What do you mean, Eulalia? "

" What I say, darling. Dick's a man of several facets
—no specialist! Thank the Lord! "

" Her habit of covering up her mouth with her
hand when not speaking isn't exactly pretty."

" She needs debarbarising, of course."

" She'd still be black, Eulalia! "

" Black or no, she's certainly perfectly beautiful."

" She may appeal to your epicurism, dear, although
she mayn't to mine."

" She was telling me—only fancy, Lizzie—that
the peacocks in her land are much bigger——! "

" I should think they were, Eulalia. I should imagine
they would be."

" I found her so interesting."

" I've no doubt of that, Eulalia."

" But where is she? "

Apparently, like the majority of persons present,
she had sauntered over to where a wordless passional
play performed by mixed religious seemed to be
scoring a hit.

On an overt stage ranged beneath the walls of
Nuestra Señora de la Pena brilliantly lit within, two pretty
probationers, Mystylia and Milka Morris, protégées
of the ladies of the house, were revealing themselves
to be decidedly promising artists, while gathered in a
semi-circle about the stage the audience was finding
occasion to exchange a thousand casuistries relative
to itself or to the crops.

There uprose a jargon of voices:

" Heroin."

" Adorable simplicity."

" What could anyone find to admire in such a shelving profile? "

" We reckon a duck here of two or three and twenty not so old. And a spring chicken *anything to fourteen.*"

" My husband had no amorous energy whatsoever; which just suited me, of course."

" I suppose when there's no more room for another crow's-foot, one attains a sort of peace? "

" I once said to Doctor Fothergill, a clergyman of Oxford and a great friend of mine, ' Doctor,' I said, ' oh, if only you could see my——' "

" *Elle était jolie! Mais jolie! . . . C'était une si belle brune . . . !* "

" Cruelly lonely."

" Leery. . . ."

" Vulpine."

" Calumny."

" People look like pearls, dear, beneath your wonderful trees."

" . . . Milka, to-night—she is like a beautiful Cosway."

" Above social littleness. . . ."

" Woman as I am! "

" Philanthropy."

" . . . A Jewess in Lewisham who buys old clothes, old teeth, old plate, old paste, old lace. And gives very good prices indeed."

" 'Er 'ealth I'm pleased to say is totally established."

" If she pays her creditors *sixpence* in the *pound* it's the utmost they can expect."

" Wonderful the Duchess of Valmouth's golden red hair, is it not? "

" ' You lie to me,' he said. ' I'm not lying, and I *never* lie,' I said. ' It's *you* who tell the lies.' Oh! I reproached him."

" I'm tired, dear, but I'm *not* bored! . . ."

" What is a boy of twenty to me? "

" It's a little pain-racked face—not that she really suffers."

Sister Ecclesia chafing at her Vows, martyred to find some outlet to expression, was like to have died, had not Nature inspired her to seek relief in her sweetest, most inconsequent way.

" I give her leave," Mère Marie de Cœurbrisé said, " to demand ' the Assembly's pardon.' "

Drawn by this little incident together, Lady Parvula de Panzoust and Mrs. Q. Comedy, a lady with white locks and face—the only creature present in a hat— —had fallen into an animated colloquy.

" These big show seats," Lady Parvula sighed, " are all alike: insanitary death-traps! "

The local land-agent's wife sent up her brows a little.

" Were you ever over Nosely? " she interjected.

" The Lauraguays'? Never! " Lady Parvula fluttered a painted fan of a bouquet of flowers by Diaz.

" My husband has the letting of it, you know."

" Ah, hah——? Well, I always admire Richard the Third, who leased his house in Chelsea to the Duchess of Norfolk for the yearly rental of one red rose."

Mrs. Comedy's mouth dropped.

" But that was hardly business! " she remarked.

" Who knows though? Perhaps it was," Lady Parvula answered, appraising her Corydon through the eyelits of her fan.

" I've a sure flair for a figure," she mused, " and this one is prodigious."

" Some say they find the country ' warping.' "

" Oh, but I feel I want to kiss you! " Lady Parvula ecstatically breathed.

" Madam? " Mrs. Comedy recoiled.

Just at this juncture, over the lawn-party, appeared

90

the truant poll-parrot of Sir Victor Vatt. Wheeling round and round the chapel cross in crazy convolutions, the bird was like something demented.

"Dear Vatt," it cried, "he is splendid: so o-ri-gi-nal: and exuberant; like an Italian Decorator. Come, Vatt! Paint me in a greenhouse . . . in a st-oove; a little exotic! . . . Where's my bloody Brush?"

"I forget," the Abbot of Up-More (a man like a sorrowful colossus) said, fingering fancifully the ring of red beard that draped his large ingenious face, "if Vatt is for us or no."

"He is to be had," Mrs. Hurstpierpoint answered. "In my private-list I have entered him as 'Shakeable': Very: he will come for a touch . . ." she added, wincing at some shooting stars that slipped suddenly down behind the house.

"As Othniel prevailed over Chushanrishathaim so ought likewise we, by self-mortification and by abstinence, to proselytise all those who, themselves perhaps uncertain, vacillate ingloriously upon the brink," the Abbot cogently commented.

With angelic humour Mrs. Hurstpierpoint swept skyward her heavy-lidded eyes.

"I thought last night, in my sleep," she murmured, "that Christ was my new gardener. I thought I saw Him in the Long Walk there, by the bed of Nelly Roche, tending a fallen flower with a wisp of bast. . . . 'Oh, Seth,' I said to Him . . . 'remember the fresh lilies for the altar-vases. . . . Cut all the myosotis there is,' I said, 'and grub plenty of fine, feathery moss. . . .' And then, as He turned, I saw of course it was not Seth at all."

"Is Seth leaving you?"

"He leaves us, yes, to be married," Mrs. Hurstpierpoint replied, acknowledging a friendly little grimace from Niri-Esther, who appeared to be comporting herself altogether unceremoniously towards Thetis Tooke over the matter of a chair.

" Nowadays, the young people sit while their elders stand! " the Abbot succinctly said, riveting a curly-pated enfant de cœur lolling coxcombically beneath the nose of a doating Statilia.

Mrs. Hurstpierpoint kicked out the fatigued silver folds of her Court train with some annoyance.

" Charlie," she beckoned.

" Here, 'm," the child chirped, coming up.

" Where's your chivalry, Charlie? Your respect to the ladies? "

The lad looked down abashed.

" Come nearer, Charlie. (Quite close, Little-Voice!) Is that ink, on your head, I see? "

" Probably. . . . Father often wipes his pen in my hair," the boy replied, darting off down a gravel path, where, having strayed away from the rest, Mrs. Tooke was dropping curtsies to the statues.

" She's loose."

" Oh! At her time? "

" Very, very loose."

The Abbot caressed his beard.

" Indeed, she looks a squilleon," he raptly conjectured.

" She's *shakeable*, Abbot, I mean: in other words one could have her . . ." Mrs. Hurstpierpoint explained.

" Ah: I see."

" My tongue is over-prone perhaps to metaphor. My cherished friend sometimes scolds me for it; only a fellow-mystic—some saint, would ever know, she says, what I'm driving at often. . . . Dear Lizzie. . . . If I could but influence her to make a Retreat; a change from Hare seems highly expedient for her; and at Arimathæa she would have still her Confessor! For something, I fear, is weighing on her mind; some sorrow she tells me nothing of; and it makes her so difficult. Just now we almost quarrelled. Yes. She grew jealous. And of a negress. Not the old one. 'Dina-dina-do.' I mean the girl in drawers. So I feel somehow Sodbury is the place for my poor angel. Just for a time. They have there, I believe, at present, Julie Bellojoso, and her sister, Lady Jane Trajane— also little Mrs. Lositer; Grouse Dubelly that was; she, of course, a fixture! . . . Thus my excellent, exquisite friend would have comradeship: and she would return here, I trust, softened, chastened, and with a less dingy outlook on life. For her talk, lately, Abbot, has been anything but bright. Indeed, she frightens me at times with her morose fits of gloom. Entre nous I lay the blame on the excellence of the garden as much as any-thing else! Our wall-fruit this year has been so very delicious; were not those dark Alphonsos perfection? Dear Father Notshort, though, forgets my wicker basket! But he was always a favourite of mine; and one hears he has great authority with the Duchess. I hope she will decide to make the plunge from Hare. Her little starveling flower-face almost makes me want to cry. I feel as if I wanted to give her straight to Jesus. She is here somewhere to-night. With her triste far look. I often say she has the instinct for dress. Even a skirt of wool with her feels to shimmer. . . . Lady Violet Logg also is somewhere about: my Poor Heart found her the other day—the day, it was, of the appal-ling storm—in *Nuestra Señora*, practically on her knees . . . and with *both* her boys." Mrs. Hurstpierpoint diffusely broke off, directing her glance towards the municipal marquee.

Emerging from it amid a volley of laughter, came a puny, little old, osseous man of uncertain age, brandishing wildly to the night an empty bottle of Napoléon brandy.

"Ho! broder Teague," his voice flew forth, "dost hear de decree?

"Lilli burlero, bullen a-la.
Dat we shall have a new deputie,
Lilli burlero, bullen a-la.
Lero lero, lilli burlero, lero lero, bullen a-la,
Lero lero, lilli burlero, lero lero, bullen a-la.

Ara! but why does he stay behind?
Lilli burlero, bullen a-la.
Ho! by my shoul 'tis a protestant wind.
Lilli burlero, bullen a-la.
Lero lero, lilli burlero, lero lero, bullen a-la,
Lero lero, lilli burlero, lero lero, bullen a-la.

Now, now de heretics all go down,
Lilli burlero, bullen a-la.
By Chrish' and Shaint Patrick, de nation's our
own—"

But with quick insight the maître d'orchestre had
struck up a capricious concert waltz, an enigmatic, *au
delà* laden air; Lord Berners? Scriabin? Tschaikovski?
On the wings of whose troubled beat were borne
some recent arrivals.

Entering the garden from the park, they would
have reached the house, perhaps, unheeded, but for a
watchman upon his rounds.

"A fine night, Captain!" The armed protector Mrs.
Hurstpierpoint saw fit to employ against itinerant
ravishers or thieves addressed his master.

"A delicious night indeed!"

"A little rain before morning maybe . . ."

For Captain Thoroughfare had found his way home
again, anxious yet diffident enough to introduce his
bride to her new relations: while to lend a conciliatory
hand Lieutenant Whorwood himself had submitted
to pass a few days at Hare, his cajoling ways and prepossessing face having quite melted Mrs. Hurstpierpoint upon a previous visit.

And, indeed, as he lagged along in the faint boreal light behind his friend he resembled singularly some girl masquerading as a boy for reasons of romance.

He had a suit of summer mufti, and a broad-brimmed blue beaver hat looped with leaves broken from the hedgerows in the lanes, and a Leander scarf tucked full of flowers: loosestrife, meadowrue, orchis, ragged-robin.

But it was due to Thetis Tooke that their advent was first made known.

"Oh! Is it y-you, Dick?" she crooned, catching sight of her lover: "dear, is it you? Oh, Dick, Dick, Dick, my life!" She fell forward with a shattering cry.

IX

It was in the deserted precincts of a sort of Moorish palace in the purlieus of the town that Lady Parvula de Panzoust and David Tooke were to come together one afternoon some few days subsequent to the Hare-Hatch fête.

In the crazy sunlight the white embattled Kasbahs of the vast rambling villa (erected by a defunct director of the Valbay Oyster-beds, as a summer resort, towards the close of the eighteenth century) showed forcefully, albeit, perhaps, a little sullenly, above the frail giraffe-like trunks of the birch-trees, and the argent trembling leaves of the aspens, that periodically shaded the route.

"I know I should despise myself, but I don't!" Lady Parvula told herself, unrolling a bruised-blue, sick-turquoise, silk sunshade very small like a doll's. "Such perfect cant, though, with four 'honeymoons' in the hotel, to be forced oneself to take to the fields . . . ! Oh Haree-ee-ee," she flashed an œillade up into the electric-blue dome of her parasol, "why did you leave me? Why did you leave your tender 'Cowslip' by the wayside all alone? Do you hear me, Haree-ee-ee? Why did you ever leave me? And Gilda too, my girl. Oh, my darling child . . . do you know the temptation your mother is passing through? Pray for her . . . excuse her if you can. . . . We shall be like the little birds to-night. Just hark to that one: *tiara, tiara, tiara*. It wants a tiara!"

Her aphrodisiac emotions nicely titillated, Lady Parvula de Panzoust was in her element.

"The Roman bridge in Rimini, the *Long* bridge in Mantua . . ." she murmured to herself erotically, dreamily, as she crossed the Val.

She wore a dress of filmy white stuff, embroidered with bunches of pale mauve thistles, a full fichu, and a large mauve hat with wide mauve ribbons, tied in front in a large knot where the fichu was crossed on her bosom.

"Such red poppies, such blue hills and sea, I never saw!" she reflected, entering a luxurious lime alley leading to the house.

A sign-board bearing the words "commodious residence," with the name of Mr. Comedy subjoined, struck a passing chill.

Evidently he was not yet come.

"I shall scream if he turns up in a dreadful billy-cock, or plays stupid pranks," she murmured, pursing forward her lips that showed like a ripe strawberry in a face as whitened as a mask of snow.

Beneath the high trees there was a charming freshness.

"Kennst du das Land, wo die citronen blühen?" she vociferated lightly, glancing up at the sun-fired windows of the house.

"It might suit me, perhaps," she sighed, sinking down on an old green garden-seat with the paint peeling off in scales.

But to one of her impatient character expectance usually makes substantial demands upon the vitality.

"'Oui, prince, je languis, je *brûle* pour Thésée—Je l'aime,'" she lyrically declaimed.

Mightn't he be, perhaps, lurking close somewhere out of sight?

"'Laissez-moi ma main . . .'" she languidly hummed (affecting Carré in Manon).

After all there was no need, it seemed, to have put herself in quite such a hurry.

"I begin now to wish I'd worn my little bombasine," she mused, "notwithstanding the infernal quantities of hooks. It's too late to turn back for it, I suppose?

97

I feel all of a-twitter. . . . These accidental affairs . . .
I said I know I never would. I can't forget the caïquejee
on the Golden Horn; since that escapade my nerve
has gone completely. How quiet the rooks are to-day.
I don't hear any. Why aren't they chanting their
unkydoodleums? Swing high, swing low, swing to,
swing fro, swing lal-lal-lal-la. What keeps him ever?
Some horrid cow? I can't bear to think of the man I
love under some cow's chidderkins. Oh, Haree-ee-ee,
Haree-ee-ee! Why did you leave me, Henry, to this
sort of thing?"

She peered about her.

In the shade of a tree, a book, forgotten, doubtless,
by some potential tenant, was lying face downwards,
open upon the grass.

With a belief in lovers' lightest omens, Lady Parvula
de Panzoust was tempted to rise.

"*Un Document sur l'Impuissance d'Aimer*," she
pouted, pricking the brochure of Jean de Tinan with
the point of her parasol.

"I seem to receive a special warning to take steps.
. . . He may require inciting," she deliberated, dropping very daintily to a grassy slope.

The turquoise tenderness of the sky drew from her
heart a happy coo.

Overhead a wind-blown branch, upheld in its fall
by another branch below, flecked precociously, with
hectic tints, the heavy midsummer greenery.

Half sitting, half reclining, she settled herself re-
posefully against the tree-bole—limp, undefensive,
expectant.

"I shall be down to-morrow with lumbago I dare
say," the latent thought flashed through her.

Nevertheless, the easy eloquence of the pose was
worth while, perhaps, preserving.

A weasel, "with a face like a little lion," she told
herself, skipped from behind a garden dial—paused,

98

puzzled at the diaphanous whiteness of her gown,—turned tail, and disappeared briskly beneath a fissure in the plinth.

The words, "*Donec eris felix, multos numerabis amicos, Tempora si fuerint nubila, solus eris!*" traced thereon, irritated her somehow.

Pulling out a letter from her dorothy bag she beguiled the tediousness of waiting by perusing distraitly its contents.

"The *première* of Paphos," she read. "Castruccio . . . Delmé. The choruses made me weep. The Carmen Nuptiale was wholly divinely given. I fear these few months in Milan have been all in vain. My glory my voice. An old diva, a pupil of Tiejens . . . *Ah, for's e lui!* Purity of my . . . No Patti, or Pasta . . . Signor Farsetti . . . thrilling shake . . . *Caro Nome*. Lessons. Liras. One of the pensionnaires. . . . From Warsaw . . . worship . . . Mademoiselle Lucie de Cleremont Chatte. Lucie . . . Lucie . . . Lucie."

Her head flopped forward beneath her heavy hat, her apathetic eyelids closed. . . .

When at length she looked up, the fretted shadow of the house had sloped far toward the south.

Something broke the stillness.

An object that to her perplexity resolved itself into a large pink kite was being dragged slowly past her over the grass. Preceding it, the forms of Captain Thoroughfare and Niri-Esther were to be descried retreating together into the dusk. Catching itself in the garden weeds like a great maimed bird, the kite tore its way along in the wake of the insouciant pair, followed discreetly a few yards to the rear by the sorrowing figure of Thetis Tooke.

Lady Parvula was still meditating on what she had seen, when Mrs. Yajñavalkya presented herself from beneath the shade of the boskage.

Her downcast eyes and rapid respiration prepared Lady Parvula to expect the worst.

" What brings you? " she faintly asked.

" Milady P.! " the negress clasped perfervidly beneath her chin her white-gloved hands. " It is a case ob *unrequited love* . . . but dat does not mean to say you shall not be satisfied. No; oh no. On my honour."

" The affair then"—Lady Parvula de Panzoust broke a pale-veined leaf, and bit it—"proves abortive?"

" He will offer no opposition. . . . But on de other hand, he pretend he cannot guarantee to make any advance! "

Her ladyship's lip curled.

" I fear he must be cold, or else he's decadent? . . . " she said, " for I have known men, Mrs. Yajñavalkya —yes, and *many men* too!—who have found us little women the most engrossing thing in life——"

" He has abjured, he says, de female sex."

" Abjured us? Oh impossible! "

" However! he will content your caprice on one condition."

" Let me hear it."

" Marriage."

" Marriage ! ! ! ! ! "

Lady Parvula wrapped herself in her dignity.

" He seems to *me* to be an unpublished type," she said severely.

" De great, sweet slighter."

" I try to follow his train of feeling—but I can't."

" He is inhuman, milady, and dat is sure."

Lady Parvula followed absently with her glance a huge clock-beetle, exploring restively the handle to her parasol.

" At once. Where is he? " she demanded.

" I left him yonder at de gate."

" You got him to the gate! "

" And dair we just parted. 'Come along, now,' I said, ' for wif-out you I refuse to budge.' "

" Well, what made you leave him then? "

" *Kra.*"

" As he is a shy, mistrustful misanthrope . . . an inverted flower . . ."

" ' Why won't you come? ' I say to him. ' Do I ask de impossible? ' *Kra!* "

" Oh . . . I want to spank the white-walls of his cottage! "

" Vot is von misadventure."

" Do you really believe candidly there's *any* chance?"

" Dis but a hitch! "

" A disappointment, Mrs. Yajñavalkya——"

" Take what you can get, milady . . . Half a loaf is better dan no bread! Remember; and dat's vot I alvays say."

" Nonsense—; he must trot out—; I want more than crumbs."

" I get you both de crust *and* de crumb. I obtain you all you desire: only give me de time," the negress wheezed.

Lady Parvula looked malicious.

" Of course he's *stable*," she remarked.

" *Inshallah!* "

" Since seeing him in his shirt-sleeves with the peak of his cap turned over his neck, and redolent, upon the whole, of anything but *flowers* . . . he no longer thrills me," she alleged, " to the former extent."

" I could get you de cousin."

" What cousin? "

" De Bobby Jolly boy."

" . . . Too young! "

" He twelve."

" Go on! He's not eight."

" Dat child is a king's morsel."

Lady Parvula had a headshake.

101

" In the depths of the wilds you'd think young folk were bound to be more or less pent up," she reflected, in tearful tones.

Mrs. Yajñavalkya smiled beneficently.

" It is not right, my dear," she declared, " you should be bilked. . . . Vot do you say to de captain ob a ketch? Beyond de Point out dair I have in mind de very goods."

" As a rule that class is much too Esau. You understand what I mean."

" Or; have you ever looked attentively at de local schoolmaster? "

" No; I can't say I have."

" Den you certainly should! "

" A schoolmaster—there's something so very *dredged*——"

" I sometimes say to Doctor Dee he put me in mind ob Dai-Cok."

" Dai-Cok? "

" De Japanese God ob Wealth."

" Well—; I dare say he would do as a poor *pis aller*," Lady Parvula tittered, retouching her cheeks lightly with a powder-ball.

Not a breath of wind was stirring the trees. High up in the incandescent blue the whitest of moons was riding.

" Hina has lit her lamp. Hina here."

" Damnation! ! ! ! "

" Come with me now my beautiful darling. Come. Come. Be brave. Be patient," the negress begged.

Lady Parvula rose stiffly to her feet.

" I'll come perhaps a short way with you," she said, regarding speculatively the interchanging fires of the lighthouse, that revealed, far off, their illusive radiance round the Point.

" How I wish, my dear, I could bow to your wishes! "

" You? "

" Supply de need."

" I have reconsidered——" Lady Parvula breathed.
" Tell me . . . This captain of a ketch . . . Has
he . . . (There are one or two petty questions I
would like to put to you quietly as we go along . . . !) "

X

THE sky was empurpled towards the west, and the long, desolate road, winding seaward, was wrapped in shadow; and desolate, equally, was her heart.

"I loved you, Dick—: I asked for nothing better, Dear, than to be the wool of your vest . . ." Thetis softly wailed.

Her pale lips quivered.

"I would have done it yesterday," she moaned, "only the sea was as smooth as a plate!"

Yet now that it was slashed with little phantom horses it affrighted her. To be enveloped utterly by that cold stampede! Recalling the foolishness they had talked of her naiad namesake, she spat.

A fleet white pony and a little basket-wagon, with Maudie and Maidie, the charming children of Mrs. Q. Comedy, rattled by, returning from a picnic on the beach.

"I'd have blacked myself, Dick, for you. All over every day. There would have been such delight, Dear, in my aversion. . . . But you never told me your tastes. You concealed what you cared for from me. And I never guessed. . . . No; you never trusted me, Dick. . . . Besides! Everything's useless now," she soliloquised, inclining to decipher the torn particles of a letter, littering the high road beneath her feet.

Willows near Pavia——
Weeping-willows near Pavia——
Pavia University——
Pavia——

Her bruised mind sought comfort . . . (vainly) . . . amid the bits——

" Yes. Everything's useless now. For very soon, Dick, I'll be dead! "

From a bank of yellowing bracken, a beautiful cock-pheasant flew over her with a plaintive shriek.

" Dead. . . . I suppose they'll put out the Stella Maris and dredge the Bay. But the tide will bear me beyond the Point; fortunately; I'm so lightsome! Seven stone. If that . . . oh dear, oh dear. When Nellie Nackman did the same she never left the rocks. It's a matter of build purely."

Two bare-footed men—Up-Moreites—passed her with a " famished " stare.

" I have a lovely figure. Totally superior to hers. He doesn't know what I am. . . . Poor Dear. How should he? My honey-angel. . . . Oh, Dick, Dick, Dick, Dick. . . . I ought to curse you, my darling."

A labourer striding fugitively along in front of her, a young spruce-fir on his back (its bobbing boughs brushing the ground), perplexed her briefly.

" But I can't, I can't curse you, Dick. . . . Dear one, I can't. Neither, I find, can I forgive you. . . . I hope your brats may resemble their mother—that's all."

As in a stupor, forging headlong forward she was overtaken in the vicinity of Valopolis by the evening voiture of Madame Mimosa, the lady's monogram, " Kiki," wreathed in true-love-knots, emblazoning triply the doors and rear. Presumably the enchantress was returning from the parsonage there—her penchant for Canon Wertnose being well known.

Canon Wertnose, Thetis's thoughts ran on, would bury her were she to be cast ashore. The beach was considered as his " domain." . . . Canon Wertnose would call at the Farm. Her grandmother would put on her cap to receive his visit with the whiskerage appended. Canon Wertnose would caress the cat. There would be talk of Habakkuk. . . .

She started.

Seated on a mileage-stone near the road's end was Carry, the little slavey of Mrs. Yajñavalkya, her head sunk low over a book.

She had in her hands a huge bright bouquet of Chinese asters, sunflowers, chrysanthemums and dahlias, which she inhaled, or twisted with fabulous nonchalance in the air as she read. . . . She appeared to be very much amused.

" What are you laughing for, Carry Smith? " Thetis made question.

" Me? " the negress's little apprentice tittered. . . . " Oh, miss! . . . I know at last. . . ."

" What futility have you discovered now? "

" I know *at last*—about the gentlemen."

" About what gentlemen? "

" I know all about them."

" So do I—traitors."

" Oh, miss! "

" Don't be a fool, Carry Smith."

" I know, miss, about them."

" You may think you do."

" Ah, but *I know*." The child kissed her two frail hands to the first white star.

" Pick up your flowers, Carry Smith, and don't be a dilly," Thetis advised, turning from her.

Day was waning.

The retreating tide exposed to view the low long rocks, encrusting sombrely the shore. Towards the horizon a flotilla of fishing-boats showed immutable, pink-lacquered by the evening sun.

" I shall remove my hat I think," she cogitated. " It would be a sin indeed to spoil such expensive plumes. . . . It's not perhaps a headpiece that would become every one;—and I can't say I'm sorry! "

Her gaze swept glassily the deserted strand.

" It exasperates me though to think of the trouble

I gave myself over maquillage. Blanching my face and fingers (and often my neck and arms . . .) surreptitiously in the cream-cans, before their consignment to Market, when all the while," she mumbled, fumbling convulsively amid the intricacies of her veil, " he'd sooner have had me black! "

A little sob escaped her.

" Yes, he'd sooner I'd have been black," she pursued, approaching determinedly the water's brink, when, from the shade of a cruciform stone, stepped Ecclesia, the Nun.

It was her " Day."

Mingling her voice with the planing gulls, winding her way dolorously amid the harsh bare rocks, she approached Thetis Tooke as if divinely impelled.

.   .   .   .

From the grey headland, where the stone Pharos cast through the gloom its range of shimmering light, a coastguard was surprised to see two women wrestling on the beach below, their outlines dim against the western sky.

XI

CLAD in a Persian-Renaissance gown and a widow's tiara of white batiste, Mrs. Thoroughfare, in all the ferment of a *Marriage-Christening*, left her chamber one vapoury autumn day and descending a few stairs, and climbing a few others, knocked a trifle brusquely at her son's wife's door.

Through the open passage windows scent-exhaling Peruvian roses filled the long corridors with unutterable unrest, their live oppressive odour quickening oddly the polished assagais and spears upon the walls.

" Yahya? "

" It's me, dear."

" Safi? "

" May Mother come in? "

" N . . . o."

" Hurry up, then, Esther—won't you? " Mrs Thoroughfare made reply, continuing resourcefully her course towards the lower regions of the house.

A tapestry curtain depicting *The Birth of Tact*, in which *Taste* was seen lying on a flower-decked couch amid ultra-classic surroundings, divided the stairway from the hall.

" Her eye was again at the keyhole," Mrs. Thoroughfare reflected, pausing to glare at ffines, who was imparting technicalities relative to the Bridal-breakfast to his subordinates.

All was hurry and verve, making the habitual meditation in *Nuestra Señora* a particular effort to-day.

Yet, *oremus*—there being, indeed, the need.

Beyond a perpetual vigil-lamp or two the Basilica was unlit.

Glancing nervously at the unostentatious (essentially unostentatious) font, Mrs. Thoroughfare swept softly over a milky-blue porcelain floor (slightly slithery to the feet) to where her pet prie-dieu, laden with pious provender like some good mountain mule, stood waiting, ready for her to mount, which with a short sigh she did.

"Teach me to know myself, O Lord. Show me my heart. Help me to endure," she prayed, addressing a figurine in purple and white faïence by Maurice Denis below the *quête*.

Through the interstices of the be-pillared nave (brilliant with a series of Gothic banners) the sunlight teemed, illuminating the numerous *ex-votos*, and an esoteric little altar-piece of the " School " of Sodoma.

"O grant me force! " she murmured, unbending a shade at sight of the gala altar-cloth where, crumpled up amid paschal lilies and *fleurs-de-luce*, basked an elaborate frizzed lamb of her own devoted working, the smart sophisticated crown displayed by the creature ablaze with Mrs. Hurstpierpoint's unset precious stones.

"Our nuptial bouquets (hers and mine) I like to think are conserved below," she mused, laying her cheek to her hands and smiling a little wistfully towards a statue of the Virgin—*Nuestra Señora de la Pena*—standing solitary under the canopy of the apse, her heart a very pin-cushion of silver darts.

"Hail, Mary . . .! " she breathed, ignoring a decanter of sherry and a plate of herring-sandwiches —a contrivance akin to genius in drawing attention to an offertory-box near by.

From the sacristy the refined roulades of a footman (these " satanic " matches!) reached her faintly:

"Oh I'm his gala-gairle . . .
I'm his gala child,
Yes," etc.

109

Useless, under the circumstances, to attempt a *station!* "Besides," Mrs. Thoroughfare speculated, trailing her Ispahanish flounces over to the dapper, flower-filled chapel of the Salute, "I bear my own cross, God knows. . . ."

The mystic windows, revealing the astonishing Life of Saint Automona Meris, smouldered brightly.

Automona by way of prelude lolling at a mirror plein de chic, her toes on a hassock, reading a billet-doux. Automona with a purple heartsease, pursuing a nail-pink youth. Automona with four male rakes (like the little brown men of Egypt)—her hair down, holding an ostrich-fan. Automona, in marvellous mourning and with Nile-green hair, seated like a mummy bolt upright. Automona meeting Queen Maud of Cassiopia:—"You look like some rare plant, dear!" Her growing mysticism. She meets Mother Maïa: "I'm not the woman I was!" Her moods. Her austerities. Her increasing dowdiness. Her indifference to dress. She repulses her couturier: "Send her away!" Her founding of Sodbury. Her end.

"Dear ardent soul!" Mrs. Thoroughfare commented, her spirit rejoicing in the soft neurotic light.

Seldom had the Basilica shown itself as seductive.

From a pulpit festooned fancifully in prelatial purple the benediction of Cardinal Doppio-Mignoni would shortly fall.

The last time the cardinal had preached at Hare had been for the harvest festival, when a pyre of wondrous "wurzels" had been heaped so high on the pulpit-ledge that he had been almost hidden from sight. Whereupon, dislodging a layer, His Eminence had deplaced the lot—the entire structure, Mrs. Thoroughfare remembered well, rattling down like cannon-balls on to the heads of those below.

Glancing round, her eyes encountered a taper-lighting acolyte—Charlie, revolving with an air of half-cynical inquiry before a *Madeleine Lisant*, attributed to the "Master of the Passion," usually kept veiled, but to-day exposed to view.

Dipping a grimly sardonic finger in the vase of holy water by the door, Mrs. Thoroughfare withdrew, halting mechanically just outside to lend a listening ear to a confused discursive sound—the eternal *she she she* of servants' voices.

" . . . She . . . she . . ."

Through a service hatch ajar the chatter came.

" She . . ."

" There's the Blue-Room bell! "

" Confound it."

" . . . Well, dear . . . as I was saying . . . Never before was I so insulted or outraged! Just catch me taking any more topsy freedoms from her."

" I should keep my breath to cool my porridge. In your shoes, Sweetie."

" Sweetie? Who's your sweetie? . . . I'm not your sweetie."

" No? I shouldn't think you was."

" In your shoes . . . I'd put-myself-out to school, I would, and be taught some grammar! "

" Hurry up, please. . . . Come on now with the samovar—and make haste sorting the letter-bag."

" His Eminence. His Eminence: didn't some one say Cardinal Mignoni's correspondence passed first through Monsignor Girling? . . . Lord Laggard . . . Lady Laggard. Her ladyship. Her ladyship. . . . Mademoiselle Carmen Colonnade—; *do, re, mi, fa.* . . . Signora Pinpipi. The Mrs. The Mrs. . . ."

" I always know instinctive when the Mrs. has on her spiked garters."

" Do you, dear? . . . And *so* do I."

" You could hear her a-tanning herself before cock-crow this morning in her room. Frtt! but she can swipe."

" Those holly-bags, too, must tickle one's hams."

" Now her sister's visiting Valmouth, you'd have thought it was Penance enough! "

" Who are the sponsors beside Lady Laggard? "

" What's that, my dear, to you? "

" There's the Blue-Room bell again! . . ."

> " I'll be your little blue-bell
> If you'll be my little bee."

" And *don't* forget Mrs. Thoroughfare."

" . . . What Mrs. Thoroughfare? Which Mrs. Thoroughfare? . . . the white Mrs. Thoroughfare? The black Mrs. Throughfare? "

" I've seen a mort o' queer things in my day " (the voice was ffines's), " but a *negress;* oh deary me! "

· " Give me strength, my God, to bear this cross. Uphold me, Holy Mary, or I fail," Mrs. Thoroughfare inwardly breathed, retreating softly towards the drawing-room door.

The renowned room was completely bathed in sun, revealing equally the qualities and defects of the numerous baptismal or bridal gifts set out to be admired.

Bending over a charming little mirror of composite precious woods, Mrs. Thoroughfare detected Lieutenant Whorwood grooming assiduously his romantical curls.

Embarrassed at being taken thus unawares, the young man blushed up to the *rose-mauve* of his lips.

" I realise," said he, " I'm one of those who, at the last Trump, would run their hand across their hair! "

" Ah? Really—; would you? Why? "

" Probably," he replied, " because I'm naturally vain."

" I adore your hair:—and so does Dick."

" Did he say so? "

" My boy is very fond of you."

" And I'm very attached to him."

" I know you are—and that *is why* I can talk to you about my son," Mrs. Thoroughfare said, keeping the lieutenant's hand captive in her own a moment longer, perhaps, than was actually required.

" After the ceremony, I trust you'll all at length be easy."

" Their re-union in my opinion," Mrs. Thoroughfare declared, " is nothing but nonsense, but Eulalia seemed so fidgety and nervous—oh! she's so particular now about the least flaw or hitch——! And we thought it best, perhaps, to humour her."

" Those black weddings are rarely *en règle*."

" I would give the whole world willingly for the poor fellow to repudiate the affair altogether—; *get out of it!* Such a marvellous opportunity . . . But no; he's utterly infatuated by his wife, it seems;—too much, alas, I fear . . ."

" Dear Mrs. Thoroughfare," the lieutenant sympathetically said, " don't think I can't understand. I do . . . absolutely."

Mrs. Thoroughfare looked appreciative.

" I wish I was more stoic, Lieutenant Whorwood," she replied, " I wish I had less heart. . . . But I'm super-sensitive. So I suffer like a fool! "

" It isn't my business of course," he said, " to meddle in souls. But Father Colley-Mahoney should be skilled to advise."

" I've an inkling that Father very soon may be resigning his post," Mrs. Thoroughfare returned. " Such a pity! None of the chaplains ever stay long. . . . They seem to dislike Eulalia hauling them out of bed o' nights to say Midnight Masses for her."

" But *does* she? " the lieutenant murmured, ensconcing himself in an easy-chair.

" Oh, my dear, she's merciless. . . . Eulalia's in-

exorable. . . . Dom Jonquil, Père Ernest des Mar-
telles, she wore them *out*. You're aware of course
about THE KING . . ."

" The old story? "

" For Eulalia with her glowing artist mind—she is
a born artist—she reminds me often of Delysia—it is
anything but ' old.' Her poor spirit, I fear, is ever-
lastingly in the back of the Royal Box that ghastly
evening of Pastor Fido: or was it in a corner of it she
was? She is so liable to get mixed."

" I understand at any rate she projects presenting
Mrs. Richard herself at one of the coming courts."

" Oh she's very full of plans—although she tells
me none of them now."

" She has been consulting me instead! "

" You remind her of a pet *cicisbeo* she had on her
wedding tour—so she pretends."

" She designs a trip to Paris, and to Vienna too, and
Rome; and she has a wild delicious scheme even of
visiting *Taormina*."

" She'll be all over the place now I suppose. I
shouldn't wonder if she didn't marry again."

" It's for little Mrs. Richard presumably that she
goes."

" It's ridiculous how she spoils her. But it's useless
to remonstrate. One would have thought she'd have
shaved her head and put on mourning. One would
have thought she would have received her death-
blow. I've known her to take to her bed for a mere
black-beetle. Yes, oh, I have . . . blubbering and
lamenting like a great frightened silly. But for a hulk-
ing *black* savage! not a bit of it! She enjoys all the
kudos of a heathen's conversion (a ' double conversion,' as she says, on account of the child) and forgets
altogether the discreditable connection."

" It's really not such a discreditable one after all."

" I'll refuse to believe this little madcap negress

was ever born a Tahaitian princess. No, Lieutenant Whorwood, or that Mrs. Yajñavalkya of Valmouth is only her nurse."

" At Tarooa we knew quite well the brother—the banana man . . . employed on King Jotifa's estate."

" Beuh! "

" The bride's credentials anyway will probably be examined; as Mrs. Hurstpierpoint declares she shall know ' no rest ' until she has secured for her *the precedence of the daughter of an earl.*"

" Through the Laggards' wire pulling, I wonder."

" He's vastly struck by her."

" She provokes him. . . . He finds her piquant."

" If only she wouldn't run at one quite so much and rumple one's hair! "

" Last night after dinner when *we* all withdrew she amused herself by smacking the hermaphrodite. . . . So Eulalia's full of hopes, she says, that she will sometimes take a hand with the broom. . . ."

" She made a sudden dash for my b-t-m. Greatly to my amazement."

" Oh, she's a regular puss; my word she is! A regular *civet* if ever there was," Mrs. Thoroughfare wickedly commented.

" She's perhaps a little too playful."

" Having torn to piecemeal Eulalia's copy of *Les Chansons de Bilitis* and ' mis-used ' my set of dear Dumas the Elder, one might say in truth—she was destructive."

" A book is anathema to her."

" Even a *papier poudré* one; for when I gave her my little precious volume, my little inseparable of *blanc de perle* in order to rub her nose, she started grating her teeth at me—to my utter terror! Rolling her eyes; lolling out her tongue——"

" One has to feel one's way with her."

" I'm sure I meant it kindly! "

" A negress never powders."

" Why not? "

" Because she *knows* it's useless," the lieutenant lucidly explained.

" Her chief pleasure she seems to find in digging about among the coco-nut fibre in the conservatory with her hands."

" She's very fond of gardening."

" And she is also very fond, I fear, of betel. Yes, I fear my boy is married to a betel-chewer. But of course *that* is nothing. . . . ' De worst ob dis place,' she said to us last night, ' is dat dair is no betel! No betel at all;—not ob any discription! ' ' Are you a betel-chewer, then, my dear? ' I asked, *aghast.* ' Oh yes,' she answered without winking. ' How I do crave for some.' "

" It's likely to be injurious to her babe at present."

" *Which?* She's expecting a second enfantement, you know, immediately . . . Oh she's such a quick puss."

" A prettier, more câline mite than Marigold I never saw."

Mrs. Thoroughfare exchanged a quick glance with heaven.

" It's a pity the servants don't think so," she said, " for none of them will go near her! Baby has had three nurses in one fortnight; not that she perhaps is altogether to blame. The new woman, Mrs. Kent, that came only yesterday (I got her too through the columns of 'Femina') Eulalia seems all against. She can't ' abide' her, in fact, as they say in Papiete."

" So soon? "

" Oh Eulalia's so difficult. And she goes far too much to the Nursery. . . ! And unfortunately she isn't *mealy-mouthed.* . . . Eulalia says what she thinks," Mrs. Thoroughfare murmured, her voice discreetly sinking as an old maid-servant of the house peered into the room—ostensibly only to sneeze twice— and out again.

"It disturbs her," the young man ventured, "that you don't get on better with Mrs. Dick!"

Mrs. Thoroughfare's eyes wandered ruefully to a superlatively sensitive miniature—one of the numerous wedding-gifts—portraying Niri-Esther, radiant with wax-white cheeks, as seen through the temperament of a great artist.

"There'd be more affection, perhaps, between us," she returned sadly, "if she resembled that."

"It's rather a gem— Who did it?"

"Sir Victor . . ."

"It's quite inspired!"

With pensive precision Mrs. Thoroughfare drew on a pair of long, primrose-tinted gloves.

"To surprise Eulalia," she murmured, "I've commissioned him—only don't let it go further—to compose a Temptation of Saint Anthony for *Nuestra Señora*, a subject she has ever been fond of, it being so full of scope. He proposes inducing the local Laïs, Madame Mimosa, to pose as the Temptation: but I say, she isn't seductive enough. . . . No 'Temptation': at least, *I* shouldn't find her one."

"But why be dull and conventional; why be banal; why should you have a female model?"

"Why, what else, Lieutenant," Mrs. Thoroughfare shifted a cameo bangle dubiously from one of her arms to the other, "would you suggest?"

"Oh! A thousand things . . ." the lieutenant was unprecise.

"No; if he can't find a real temptation, a proper temptation, an irresistible temptation—I shall put him 'off' with a little flower-piece, some arrangement, perhaps, of *flame-coloured roses* and tell Eulalia it's the 'Burning Bush.'"

"The Nation should prevent his old Mother from leaving the country."

"Oh . . . why? What has she done?"

" Nothing—His masterpiece I meant."

" I understood him, once, I think, to say that *that* was the *Madame Georges Goujon with Arlette and Ary.* . . ."

" Oh he has so many. His drawing of a Valmouther getting over a stile is something I could covet."

" They say his study of the drawer of the Bawd's Head Hostelry here is worthy of Franz Hals," Mrs. Thoroughfare related.

But the entry of Mrs. Hurstpierpoint bearing a long-clothes baby put an end to the colloquy.

Out of courtesy to the bride, and perhaps from some motive of private thanksgiving, her face was completely covered by a jet-black visard. Big beaded wings rose from her back with a certain moth-like effect.

" Tell me, Elizabeth," she asked, " will I do? "

" Do! ! Eulalia—I never saw anything like you."

" I hope the dear Cardinal won't tell me I'm unorthodox; or do you think he will? "

" Take it off, Eulalia," Mrs. Thoroughfare begged.

" I shall not, Elizabeth! "

" Take it off! "

" No."

" But why should you conceal yourself behind that odious mask? "

" I wear it, dear, only because a white face seems to frighten baby," Mrs. Hurstpierpoint explained.

" Eulalia, Eulalia."

" Mind, Elizabeth. . . . Be careful of my wings."

" You're beyond anything, Eulalia."

Mrs. Hurstpierpoint sat down.

" Sister Ecclesia has just been giving me an account, in dumb show, of the young woman whom she saved from drowning. . . . But for her the sea would have absorbed her. . . . However, she is now comfortably installed in the Convent of Arimathæa, and already shows, it seems, signs of a budding vocation! So peradventure she will become a Bride of the Church."

" Let us hope so, anyway. But talking of ' brides,'
Eulalia, *where's Esther?* "

" She was outside, dear, a moment ago. . . ."

" In *toilette de noce?* "

" And so excited! She's just floating in happiness
—floating, swimming, sailing, soaring, flying. The
darling! She is happy. So hap-py! Oh——"

" Really, dear, it's you that seem elated."

" Your boy has my condemnation, Bessy; but he
has also my forgiveness," Mrs. Hurstpierpoint blandly
declared.

" Oh! Eulalia, you're too subtle for me."

" Call her in, darling, do, or she may perhaps take
cold, and a bride ought not to do that. I had such a
cold on *my* honeymoon I remember, I never really
ceased sneezing."

" Oh, she'll come in I dare say when she wants to,
Eulalia."

" You amuse me, Eliza. . . . What makes you so
unaccommodating? "

" It's odd you should ask, Eulalia! "

" Our friendship is unalterable, my little Lizzie,
nothing has changed, or come between."

" Mind Marigold, Eulalia."

" What is it she wants? I expect it's her bobo! "

" No she doesn't, Eulalia. She doesn't want it at
all."

" Esther has no notion yet of managing a child. . . .
Although she appears to have any number of quixoti-
cisms."

" I fear we shall find she has her own little black
ideas about everything, Eulalia."

" Well, well; if she has, she must drop them."

" Naturally," the lieutenant interposed, " her intellectual baggage is nil—simply nil," he added, lighting complacently a cigarette.

" Father wouldn't agree with you there at all; and

he has had her, remember, daily, for pious Instruction."

" I fear, Eulalia, she was won as much as anything by our wardrobe of stoles."

" Father seems half in awe of her. . . .' Is an *egregious* sin a *mortal* sin? ' she asked him quite suddenly the other day."

" Oh! Eulalia! "

" She's devoted, though disrespectful, he tells me," Mrs. Hurstpierpoint murmured, blowing a kiss to the bride who was passing the windows just then.

" Rain fell steadily in the night; the grass must be drenched."

" Oh, Esther—your feet."

" When the Spina-Christi sheds its leaves my God what sorrow and stagnance," Mrs. Thoroughfare sighed oppressed.

" Shall you want the horses, do you think, this evening, Elizabeth? "

" I don't want them, Eulalia."

" Are you sure, Elizabeth? "

" Perfectly, Eulalia."

" The evening drive is almost an institution of the past. . . ."

Mrs. Thoroughfare assented.

" Here we are too with winter upon us," she observed.

" Yes; and this is not the Tropics, my mignonne Niri! " Mrs. Hurstpierpoint reminded her convert as she came forward into the room.

" In de winter," the negress lisped, " our trees are green wif parrots."

" Are they, my dear? "

" Green! "

" Think of that now, dear child."

" Green wif dem."

" Did you hear, Elizabeth, what she said? "

" No, Eulalia."

" It appears their trees are never bare. Always something."

" Her salvation, in my estimate, Eulalia, should be equivalent quite to a Plenary-perpetual-Indulgence."

" And so *I* think too."

" Had she been more accomplished: wives should second their husbands; if not, perhaps, actually lead them. . . ."

" She does not want abilities, I can assure you, Eliza. She knows how to weave grasses. She can make little mats. She's going to teach me some day; aren't you, Esther? She and I are going to make a mat together. And when we've made it, we'll spread it out, and kneel down on it, *side by side;* won't we, Esther? "

" Yaas! " the negress answered, fondling playfully the Hare hermaphrodite.

" You may look, dear, but don't touch. Esther! Pho pet. My *dear*, what next? "

" There's a mean in all things . . . really."

" Giddy."

" Incorrigible."

" You must learn to recollect yourself, dear child, or else I shall return the Lord Chamberlain our Cards." Mrs. Hurstpierpoint made show of rising.

" Oh, she'd better be presented in Ireland, Eulalia. Dublin Castle to *begin* with—afterwards we'll see ——!! "

" Ireland? "

" What do you say, Lieutenant Whorwood? "

The lieutenant laid whimsically his face to a long cylindrical pillow of cloth of silver garnished with beaded-flowers.

" What do *I* say? " he echoed, half closing his eyes and flicking the cigarette-end from his knees, when a discharge of bells from *Nuestra Señora*, and the arrival of the vanguard of the bridal guests, prevented further discussion.

" Her Grace, the Duchess of Valmouth; the Honourable Mrs. Manborough of Castle Malling " — ffines' voice filled the room.

" You shall hold Baby, Lieutenant, while I——" Mrs. Hurstpierpoint flapped expressively her loose-winged sleeves.

" Sir William West-Wind, Mr. Peter Caroon, Mrs. Trotter-Stormer, Sir Wroth and Lady Cleobulina Summer-Leyton, Sir Victor Vatt, Master Xavier Tanoski, Lady Lucy Saunter, Miss à Duarté, Miss Roxall, Lady Jane Congress, Lady Constance Cadence-Stewart, Mrs. Q. Comedy, Lady Lauraguay, Lady Lukin de Lukin, Mrs. Lumlum, Mr. Argrove, Mrs. Lositer, General George Obliveon, Lady Parvula de Panzoust."

Exhaling indescribably the esoteric gentillezze of Love, she was looking almost girlish beneath a white beret de Picador, enwreathed with multifarious clusters of silken balls, falling behind her far below the waist. Wearing a light décolleté day-dress, her figure since her previous visit to Hare had perceptibly grown stouter.

She was eyeing her hostess with wonder unrestrained when a dowager with a fine film of rouge wrapped in many shawls sailing up to her said:

" Persuade my sister do to take off her mask. Can't you persuade her to doff it? "

Lady Parvula dimpled.

" If you, Arabella, can't—why how," she returned, " should I? "

Lady Laggard shook censoriously her shawls.

" I fear," she observed, " my poor sister will be soon a *déclassée*. She has been a sore grief to us—a sad trial! But when she begged me to be a godmother to the little Aida, I could hardly say no."

" Cela va sans dire."

" Her escapade with King Edred was perfectly disgraceful! She got nothing out of him, you know, for anyone—like the fool that she was. And to see her to-day going about be-winged, be-masked . . ."

" Sad, isn't it, how the old Hare days seem completely gone: vanished."

" She conceals her upper-lip, one must allow," Lady Laggard commented. " But there was no—or *next* to no—was there—to *speak* of—about the eyes? . . . And nothing, nothing to excuse all that long fall of dreary lace."

" Really she looks so quaint I can hardly help laughing," Lady Parvula declared.

" She must be bitterly mortified, I imagine, by this marriage."

" It shows though, I think, her savoir faire, to put the best construction on it."

" The old Noblesse—where is it now? "

" Ah! I wonder."

" With a woman like that his career is closed."

" You may be sure they'll soon be separated! "
Lady Laggard removed an eyelash.

" They're not really married yet, you know," she alleged.

" N . . . o? "

" The ceremony before I gather was quite null and void."

" In . . . deed? "

" Their own rites, so it seems, are far far simpler. All they do is *simply* to place each a hand to the torso of the Beloved. And that's as far—will you *believe it*, dear?—as we are at present! "

" Your sister spoke of ' special licence.' "

" She would; she has the tongue of a Jesuit."

" I didn't of course realise . . ."

" We were pumping the bride, Lord Laggard and

I, and she told us, poor innocent, she was not married yet," Lady Laggard averred, shaking long tremulous earrings of the time of Seti II of Egypt.

"I notice she likes lights and commotion, which goes to show she has social instincts!"

"Well, it's some time I suppose since there's been a negress——"

"All the fair men—the blondes, she will take from us. . . ."

"I wish I'd a tithe of your charms, dear."

"But I don't really mind! . . . So long as *I* get the gypsies. . . ."

"They should forbid her from repeating a horrid equivocal epigram of old Dr. Dee's—on the Masseuse, La Yajñavalkya."

"What was it, Arabella?"

"*Her brains are in her arms.*"

"And are they?"

"I don't know, dear, where they are. Such a pity *hers* aren't anywhere. Her incessant 'Wot for dis?' gets so on my nerves."

"I don't wonder. It would on mine. I'm such a nervous woman! Now I've no Haree-ee-ee to look after me I get so fluttered. . . ."

"All these priests in the house I find myself a strain. The old Cardinal, with his monstrous triple-mitre, one goes in terrors of. He was in the passage just now as I came through waiting for someone. And last night—there's only a panel door between our rooms —I heard him try the handle."

"Their last chaplain—Père Ernest—I remember was a danger. A perfect danger! He could have done anything with me, Arabella, had he willed. I was plastic wax with him."

"With their faggots of candles (and their incense) they seek to render imbecile our poor sex. Coming by Nuestra, I assure you, I was almost *poisoned*. Or, to use a juster metaphor, perhaps," Lady Laggard corrected herself, " suffocated," she added, " by the fumes."

" Monsignor Vanhove, Father O'Donoghue, Frater Galfrith, Brother Drithelm, Père Porfirio "—ffines insistently continued in his office until, in sweeping purple and scarlet biretta, Cardinal Doppio-Mignoni himself passed valedictionally through the rooms.

In the extravagant hush, following on his transit, a prolonged peacock's wail sounded electrifying from the park: *Nijny-Novgorod, Nijny-Novgorod*—creating among the younger bridesmaids an impression of " foreboding."

Only Mrs. Hurstpierpoint, to judge by her rich enveloping laugh, seemed really happy or serene.

" I always intended to visit *Walt Whitman*, didn't I, Lizzie? Poor old Walt! . . . I wrote: ' Expect me and my maid . . . . I'm coming! ' I said. . . . It was the very spring he died."

Involving some interesting, intellectual trips, she was descanting lightly to right and left.

" I remember you intended once to visit me," the Bolshevik member for Valmouth, Sir William West-Wind, softly remarked.

" You, Sir William? And when did I ever intend to visit you, I wonder? "

" There was a time," Sir William murmured, "when I confess I expected you."

" Have you any intention, Eulalia," a *douairière* inquired, " of visiting the present châtelaine of Nosely? "

" You dear angel—I wasn't aware even it was let."

" To a field-marshal's widow."

" My brother," one of the bridesmaids giggled, " was his favourite *aide-de-camp*."

" And what is *she* like? "

" He describes her as lissom as a glove, lively as a kid, and as fond of tippling as a Grenadier-Guard."

" She sounds a treasure," Mrs. Hurstpierpoint declared, with a glance backward over her wings.

" Go to Vivi Vanderstart—and say I sent you! " the Duchess of Valmouth was saying.

" Very well, dear, I will."

" Her boast is, she makes only ' Hats for Happy Women.' "

" I always pin my faith in Pauline Virot. . . ."

" One should pin one's faith only in God," Mrs. Hurstpierpoint commented blithely.

" Only where, Eulalia? "

" Only with Him."

" I remember," Mrs. Thoroughfare dryly laughed, " when Eulalia's God was *Gambetta*."

" Gambetta, Betty—what next will you say, naughty, naughty angel? "

But what Mrs. Thoroughfare subsequently would have said was lost amid Church canticles.

It was the call to the altar.

Oscillating freely a long chain incense swinger, a youthful server, magnificent in white silk stockings and Neapolitan-violet maroquin shoes, presented himself on the threshold in a fragrant veil of smoke.

Venite.

Followed by Charlie with the Holy Pyx and by Father Colley-Mahoney and various officiating priests, he traversed from end to end, amid much show of reverence (crossing and crouching), the vast salon.

' Grant she shall find,"

(Pinpipi with her great male voice from " Nuestra " was waking the echoes beyond)

" On Yniswitrins altars pale,
  The gleaming vision of the Holy Grail."

126

" Yes; grant Lord her *soul* shall find," Mademoiselle Carmen Colonnade, the beloved of the Orpheum, Scala, San Carlo, Costanzi, simultaneously (more, or less) struck in, her soft vocal flourishes and pimpant variations soaring, baby-like, high above the strong soprano voice of the severe Pinpipi.

> " *'Es, gwant 'Ord 'er 'oul*—
> Grant it shall find—
> *On Ynis-wi-trins walters*—
> Altars—
> WALTERS PALER!
> The gleaming vision—
> —*dazzling*—
> Of—
> *The Holy Grail-a!* "

" Come, Esther," Mrs. Hurstpierpoint murmured, dashing a tear from her mask.

" Yield the *pas* to a negress! *Never!* " Lady Laggard looked determined.

" Oh, Eulalia! " Mrs. Thoroughfare touched her arm.

" You dear queen."

" Have you seen my boy, Eulalia? "

" No, Elizabeth—; not to-day."

" No one can find him."

" Ah les oiseaux amoureux," Mrs. Hurstpierpoint began a series of seraphic giggles, "chers oiseaux . . . paradise uccellinis . . . delicious vogels. . . ."

" I feel half-worn-out."

" Come, Esther child, to church! "

But Niri-Esther had run out of the house (old, grey, grim, satanic Hare) into the garden, where, with her bride's bouquet of malmaisons and vanessa-violets, she was waywardly in pursuit of—a butterfly.

FAREWELL